W9-BDL-897

WITHDRAWN
Anne Arundel Co. Public Library

PRAISE FOR *I KEEP MY WORRIES IN MY TEETH*

"By sinking its teeth into the absurd core of everyday life, Anna Cox's extraordinary debut achieves a remarkable feat: it offers a meditation on the nature of time, loss, and solitude, while also being outrageously funny."

—Hernan Diaz, author of *In the Distance*

"As comic as it is moving, Anna Cox's *I Keep My Worries in My Teeth* introduces a fresh new voice."

—Gary Shteyngart, author of *Lake Success*

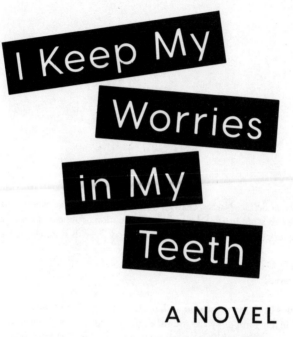

I Keep My Worries in My Teeth

A NOVEL

ANNA COX

Little
a

This is a work of fiction. Names, characters, organizations, places, events, and incidents are either products of the author's imagination or are used fictitiously. Any resemblance to actual persons, living or dead, or actual events is purely coincidental.

Text copyright © 2020 by Anna Nester Scalf Cox
All rights reserved.

No part of this book may be reproduced, or stored in a retrieval system, or transmitted in any form or by any means, electronic, mechanical, photocopying, recording, or otherwise, without express written permission of the publisher.

Published by Little A, New York

www.apub.com

Amazon, the Amazon logo, and Little A are trademarks of Amazon.com, Inc., or its affiliates.

ISBN-13: 9781542044530 (hardcover)
ISBN-10: 1542044537 (hardcover)
ISBN-13: 9781542043076 (paperback)
ISBN-10: 1542043077 (paperback)

Cover design by Micaela Alcaino

Printed in the United States of America

First edition

For my brothers, who taught me how to laugh.

OHIO, 1979

RUTH STANHOPE

In another time, I would have been an alchemist, but in 1979 people buy their gold at the mall, so I perform a different kind of magic. I transform negatives into positives.

I own Vixen Photography, and my business is looking at your business. My customers carry the pyramids in their pockets and tuck the fiery sun beneath their pillows. In a photograph, distance disappears and past fuses to present; it's time travel, on the cheap. No ticket, no passport. Stop a rocket with your pinkie, hold a flame and never blister. Portable enchantment, rolled up and lighttight.

I own three stores: one by the Great Lake, one in the mall, and the original store, across from the Juliet Pencils factory. All the shops were built to resemble their foxy namesake: the buildings have burnt sienna bodies and bushy twelve-foot tails encircling their haunches. The business name is a feminine twist on the British inventor of photography, William Henry *Fox* Talbot. Fox Talbot announced his discovery around the same time as a Frenchman, Louis Daguerre, and even though the French try to claim ownership, photography's invention is a combination of simultaneous discoveries and parallel mistakes. The French call that a mélange. Here in Ohio we just say *mutt*.

The Vixen architecture is eye-catching, but the most unique part of each store is the camera obscura built into the fox's body. A camera obscura is a simple darkened room with a small hole in the wall.

The hole acts like a lens and projects the outside world inside. When camera obscuras first appeared in the thirteenth century, people mistook them for sorcery because the outside world was pulled inside and turned upside down. First-time visitors to the Vixen camera obscura don't expect familiar people and places to look so unfamiliar once they are inverted. I explain that they are seeing the world as it is, but no one believes me, not even after I remind them that images come into the eye upside down; and by the time I explain the function of the optic nerve and emphasize that *what you think you see and what you actually see are vastly different* . . . most customers have wandered off or interrupted me to ask for coupons. Seeing the world upside down should make people feel realigned, but it doesn't, and I don't blame them, not really. Accepting the illusion of the right-side-up world is easier than accepting that seeing isn't believing.

The camera obscura needs daily maintenance, and three decades ago when I opened my first store, I could lie on the floor, check image sharpness, and bounce to my feet without thinking. I didn't marvel at my steadiness because assuming norms are normal is the hubris of youth. Now I need a bit of help, not enough that people notice but enough that I do. Most of my life I took the stairs two at a time, but now I wrap my hand around the banister and watch my feet while I climb.

I work at all three Vixen locations, and this morning I'm at the shop across from the Juliet Pencils factory. This location has the largest camera obscura, and its curved walls offer a panoramic view of the factory and the adjacent park. Every few months I have the walls repainted because the fresher the walls, the more they resemble a movie screen. The room's privacy and movie-theater darkness make it a popular make-out place for teens. I have a damp sponge for wiping sneaker prints and phone numbers off the wall. In the center of the room is a Naugahyde bench where visitors can sit and admire the view, and about once a week, I have to turn the bench over and pry off hunks of chewed gum.

The camera obscura requires an external point for checking and maintaining focus, and at this location I use the neon sign on the roof of Juliet Pencils—a yellow pencil that declares: **JULIET PENCILS MAKE YOU WRITE!** The sign has been skywriting for generations, and it's large enough to be visible from the edge of the county. Most days the yellow pencil pops against the blue sky, but this morning the focus is fuzzy, so I open the panel and adjust the aperture as a crow flies across the wall, its body flat like a child's drawing, a swooping *m*. The bird soars across my chest, down my pant leg, and then disappears under the door.

Now that the world is sharp again, it's time to open the store. I walk to the front of the shop and flip the sign to **OPEN**. Most of the morning I sell fresh film, accept development orders, and return glossy prints. In between customers, I monitor the chemistry levels in the color processor and prep black-and-white film for development. The camera obscura is reserved by the hour, and when the eleven o'clock appointment arrives, I take her to the room and suggest that she sit on the bench until her eyes adjust. She's excited to see the world upside down, so I don't think there will be any issues, but as I close the door, I let her know I'll be up front if she needs anything.

Ten minutes later she finds me and tells me the room is filling with smoke.

ESTHER SPARK

I keep my worries in my teeth.

Tooth 1: Black ice and banana peels in front of bear traps.

Tooth 2: Having a baby.

Tooth 3: Not having a baby.

Tooth 4: Dying. Not the dying part of dying, when the triangles of the beep-beep-beep machine shrug their shoulders and slump into a straight line. I'm okay with that, but I'm not okay with people standing around my hospital bed, pointing and whispering because I was too worried about dying to pluck my chin hairs.

Some of my teeth are reserved for long-term worries like nuclear annihilation, finding shoes that are comfortable but not ugly, or a clerical error that forces me to repeat high school. Others are reserved for temporary worries, but the one worry that unites both bicuspids and incisors is the fear of getting knocked out. I can't live without my teeth because, if I lose my teeth, I'll lose my job at Juliet Pencils, and losing my job would be a disaster because my mouth is the only place the world makes sense.

I was an anxious kid with angry gums. Birch bark, tire tread, clay pots, and silky cat paws—if I wanted to calm myself, I opened my mouth and shoved it in. When I teethed, I refused the cold comfort of frozen washcloths and instead gnawed on golf clubs, a habit my hopeful parents misinterpreted as budding athletic talent, but my chubby fingers weren't as strong as my stumpy teeth. Mom tired of nosy neighbors sending social workers who pursed their lips at my black eyes, so she bought me tiny sunglasses and locked the golf bag in the garage. Bedtime meant stories and stuffed animals, but I bit Teddy's arm and aspirated stuffed-bear stuffing. Penicillin cleared my lung infection, but Teddy had to live on a high shelf, so I learned to cuddle rolling pins and vacuum cleaner hoses.

When my permanent teeth arrived I got fat, fast. Tests ruled out glandular problems, and dentists questioned the excessive wear on my molars, but no one knew what to do, so Mom enrolled me in ballet classes, and after six months my pliés and tendus were still wooden, but I lost weight because the other girls taught me how to eat without eating. After days of Tab and celery sticks, the skeleton girls permitted themselves one treat—a snack-size bag of potato chips, usually sour cream and onion, occasionally barbecue—to be shared among all twelve of them. After their coat-hanger fingers slipped into the oily bag, the girls assembled in a tight circle and closed their eyes. On the count of three (we were learning waltzes) the dressing room filled with quiet chewing, rustling tutus, and sour cream exhales. When the fatty juice threatened to slip down their throats and pad their forked hips, the girls bourréed to the trash can and spat, spat, spat until their mouths were sour-cream-and-onionless. Water was passed, everyone swished, and discipline was restored. I didn't care about *Swan Lake*, but chewing without swallowing, understanding without possession or consumption, that was life-changing stuff.

At my last checkup, the dentist poked me with his shiny stick, snapped his glove, and said, *You have the gums of an eighty-year-old.*

The exam light shined in my eyes, and I used my hand as a shield. *I'm not eighty.*

I'm not twenty either. I'm in that late-thirties zone where gums are puffier and dreams deferred. The dentist fitted me for a nocturnal appliance. That was his word: *appliance.* I don't like that word. It makes me think of deep freezers, like I'm sleeping with a melon baller in my mouth. The dentist patted my knee and told me the appliance was for my own protection. I don't like that word either. *Protection* makes me think of belted sanitary pads, and that makes me angry or it makes me want to cry, but either way I want cake. The first night I slept with the appliance was like shoving cold cereal into my soft palate, but now I'm used to it. It helps my teeth relax, and relaxed teeth are precise teeth, and thanks to my protective appliance, my mandibular control is better than ever, exact to 0.0000008 mm, which makes me the best MouthFeel Tester™ and VIP Pencil Preserver™ Juliet Pencils has ever employed.

If it were up to my teeth, I'd work seven days a week, because exercising my teeth exorcises my worries. After a few days without work, my longtime fears and temporary worries escape their craggy homes and battle for dominance. Holidays are the worst. My jaw throbs, my teeth threaten recession, I threaten dentures, they threaten mutiny, and everyone yells at each other, until the only thing that calms us down is rum with a Tab chaser. I can't imagine my life without my job at Juliet Pencils, and luckily I don't have to because no one can do what I do, and the factory is so successful we operate three shifts a day, seven days a week, and still can't keep up with demand. We ship pencils across the country and supply all the local businesses. We sponsor the Little League team (the Points), the dance troupe (On Pointe), and the debate team (Excellent Point). The factory employs most of the town, so even if you don't work for us, you can't work without us.

Did you know that of all the things women put in their mouths, pencils are the number two most popular?

When I started at the factory, I used generic templates left by my predecessor, but after site visits with clients, I created a new system that improved customer MouthFeel by 147 percent. It's easy to confuse what I do with impersonation, but the clothes and accessories I use aren't props; my tools transport me to a toothy parallel universe where I sync with my clients' biting habits and imagine how and why they bite their pencils.

To test the MouthFeel of a legal secretary, I change into a wool skirt, a full-length slip charged with a Wednesday's worth of static cling, a blouse that looks like silk until you touch it, clip-on earrings, and nude-colored pantyhose that are too tight in the crotch and not nude enough. My manicure is chipped or smeared, or if it's near the end of the month, both. On my desk is a credit card bill I can't possibly pay, a dry-cleaning ticket for two gray wool suits (my boss's), and a thick Rolodex with his wife's birthday and his mistress's bust size. When the phone rings, I unclip one earring, cradle the receiver in the crook of my neck, pull the pencil from behind my ear, and bite. I take messages and I put clients on hold. If the person on the other end of the line is irritating, the pencil flails between my front teeth like a tiny gangplank. I transfer memoranda from Dictaphone to typewriter, and clench the pencil for the amount of time it takes to resolve a problem I didn't cause but will be blamed for anyway.

When MouthFeel testing is complete, I record observations about paint integrity, wood strength, and tongue feel, rating these on a scale from 1 (bad) to 8 (excellent). I summarize my thoughts, offer suggestions or changes, and then send the report to the head of quality control. In addition to our corporate clients, the factory has a custom-order division that produces small runs of personalized pencils. The glitter-embed option is popular, and at the end of custom-order MouthFeel testing days, I spit flecks of multicolored glitter in my bathroom sink, and even though I floss and gargle with dispatch, I wake up with gold sparkle between my teeth, as if I've spent the night bingeing on party toothpicks.

Besides MouthFeel testing, I'm also in charge of the Wall of Bite Fame, where pencils are showcased in individual glass cases, like tiny clear coffins. To prepare a pencil for the wall, I dry the VIP's spit from the barrel and then place the pencil on a velvet pad. After the pencil is sealed, the case is hung on the wall with an engraved brass plate that identifies the VIP by name and profession. I don't need to read the nameplates because bite patterns mirror personalities. Henry Kissinger crushed his brass eraser housing, Miss Ohio offered to sign her pencil with her pencil, and Karen Carpenter utilized hers in a way that the factory doesn't condone. Every year many tourists visit the Wall of Bite Fame, but most of them come to see the same two pencils. Men stare at Marilyn Monroe's scarlet lip prints and adjust their crotches, while women dream about steely sacrifice and Chanel suits as they gaze at former First Lady Jacqueline Bouvier Kennedy's pencil. Admission to the Wall of Bite Fame is free, because my boss, Juliet, believes pencils should create community.

I've worked here for nearly fifteen years, but I still remember my interview as if it happened yesterday. When the interviewer asked me, *Why would you be a good fit for this position?* I didn't know what to say, so I just answered truthfully, *I keep my worries in my teeth.* Back then, I had no idea how pencils were made, and I didn't really care, because a pencil is like air: you don't notice it until something is wrong.

Any day I bite wood is a good day, but today could be a great day because I'm biting wood on live television. Juliet created a program encouraging young women to find their life purpose in work, not boys. The program is called Girls! Do Work! It launches today with a televised factory tour lead by Juliet and her daughter, Frankie. My bicuspids and incisors are anxious because we've never been on TV, but Juliet said all we had to do was act normal and do our jobs, so I'm going to MouthFeel test like it's any other day.

My first client is Dr. Chevalier, the ophthalmologist. In the back of my office I have a closet filled with representative client outfits. For Dr. Chevalier, I slip on a charcoal pencil skirt, taupe heels, and a white lab coat that smells like an Ivy League education—freesia and aloofness. Dr. Chevalier orders pencils that mimic her patients' eye colors: espresso, moss, and window cleaner spilled in fresh snow. During allergy season she orders pencils with red graphite and peppercorn-flavored barrels. When I MouthFeel test those, my eyes burn and I sneeze a lot, but thankfully today is a standard order, so I bite and analyze: MouthFeel 8, responsive yield with a pleasant oaky aftertaste. As I make notes, my incoming-order bell chimes. I'm not expecting any new orders, so I ignore it and switch the orientation of Dr. Chevalier's pencil in order to test its rigidity from both ends.

Orders arrive in my office via a factory-wide network of glass pneumatic tubes that shuttle pencils throughout the entire manufacturing process: cutting, graphite packing, shaping and sharpening. The order bell dings again. I check the tube and it's empty. That's odd, but Juliet did mention increasing the line speed for the television coverage, so maybe the system is a bit off. I guess we're all jittery about being on TV. I flick my finger against the side of the tube. "Cut it out."

I evaluate two more pencils and then complete the paperwork for Dr. Chevalier's order. I place the tested pencils and my report into a transport container, flip the lever, and watch as it zooms across the ceiling. As I walk to my desk, the delivery bell rings again. I wonder if there's a blockage farther up the tube, in the elbow curve that's behind my wall. I crane my neck, but I can't see anything, and the bell is getting on my nerves, so I shove my arm up the tube as far as I can, and palm around inside, but I don't feel anything.

I hear tapping on the glass wall of my office. I turn around, and see Frankie smiling and waving, pointing to her watch. It's time, already? She points to my arm, the one shoved in the tube, and gives me a thumbs-up. I stick out my tongue just as Juliet and the anchorman from Channel Six News, Chuck Edmonds, approach the glass wall. Juliet points to my mouth and pantomimes biting and then points to my arm in the tube and raises her shoulders. I smile and wave, hoping that smiling and waving covers up the reality that my arm is stuck in a tube while the news anchorman stares at me. Juliet points to her watch, and the cameraman hoists the camera onto his shoulder. I yank and tug, and sweat drips into my pantyhose. I can't mess this up. I will not mess this up. I jerk my shoulder and rip my lab coat, but at least my arm is free, so I smooth my hair and walk sideways toward the camera, trying to hide my torn and dragging sleeve. I reach my desk, angle the good side of the lab coat toward the news crew, and nod to Juliet who nods to Chuck who nods to his cameraman. I force a big smile, grab a pencil without looking, and bite. The camera's light is so bright I can barely see. Chuck tilts the microphone to Juliet, and Juliet gestures in my direction and pantomimes an exaggerated bite. I don't know how long I'm supposed to do this, so I keep biting and smiling, and my eyes are itching and watering and I have to sneeze. I can't sneeze on live television. It's Girls! Do Work! not Girls! Do Sneeze! I squint and read the barrel of the pencil. It's one of Dr. Chevalier's allergy pencils. I push my palms into the steel edge of my desk. The light moves from me to Juliet and back to me as my teeth sink deeper into the pepper barrel until the pencil splinters just as the camera light shuts off. I lean forward and spit the broken pencil onto the floor and then sneeze. Through blurry eyes I see the news crew walking away, but Frankie stands in front of my glass wall, holding her neck in an invisible noose. Her eyes roll back in her head, and she sticks out her tongue. I tilt my head to the opposite side and do the same. I've known Frankie since she was a kid who got dropped off at the factory after school. If I ever have a kid, I want it to be like Frankie. She gives in first, laughing, and then kisses her palm and smacks it against the glass wall before she runs to catch up with her mother and the news crew.

FRANKIE ROSENBLUM

If I had known the last thing I'd ever say to my mom would be a dumb joke about nuns, I would have worked harder on my nun impression. After three years at St. Lucy's All Girls Preparatory Academy, I should have had a better gag than a dishtowel tied around my head. Other high schools have boys and football fields, but St. Lucy's has a forty-foot statue of a blind saint facing a reflecting pool, like the Washington Monument, but smaller and stuck in Ohio. My favorite days are when birds shit on her stony head.

St. Lucy is a saint because she plucked out her eyes with a fork. You've probably seen the Gothic paintings of her, the fair-haired virgin holding her eyes on a golden plate? Blind people pilgrimage to the St. Lucy statue because she once wept a peppermint-flavored tear, and around here that counts as a miracle. Everyone in town knows the miracle was actually a homecoming prank. One football team, wads of red-and-white swirly peppermints, and an unexpected rain. We aren't allowed to speak the truth because the St. Lucy's gift shop supports the school by selling eye-shaped mints. Blind pilgrims pay a lot of money to climb a ladder and lick Lucy's eye sockets, then return to their tour buses and hope for a minty miracle. Students aren't allowed to lick her, but we've all heard the rumors: her sockets smell like tuna, and they're smooth like pudding skin.

The Sisters of St. Lucy collect data on every visiting pilgrim, so I've learned a lot about blindness. Some people are born blind, but other people gradually lose their sight from an eye disease or from the recent spike in fondue-related blindings (sharp stick, hot cheese, unexpected sneeze). People who are born blind accept their blindness, but people who lose their sight slowly have trouble adjusting because their blindness approaches like fog rising from a lake, obscuring family faces and falsely padding life's architecture: table edges, staircases without banisters, forks. The data surprised me because I thought people with more time to adjust would be better adjusted, but I guess if that were true I'd be used to my mom wearing buttons about women needing men like fish need bicycles. I'd also be used to her telling me I need to peer into my cervix and raise my consciousness.

Why do the two weirdest things have to happen on the same day? Mom's Girls! Do Work! rally and St. Lucy's vocation day, when all students, even curly-haired Rosenblums like me, are supposed to listen for an invitation from God to join the convent. I don't want to be a teen-bride of God any more than I want to be my mother; but unlike God, my mother can ground me.

Mom is on a health kick, so this morning instead of Crunch Berries cereal there's breakfast gruel. I grab a dish towel and wrap it around my head like a habit and ask, "Juliet, did you schedule your rally on vocation day because you're afraid the Lord will woo me into a life of virginity and ill-fitting polyester?"

Mom ashes her cigarette and exhales. "Nice hat. Eat your breakfast."

I look at the overhead kitchen light and wonder how bugs get in the dome. "Juliet, the Lord says none of his children should have to eat this."

"Well, tell God to come down here and cook, and don't call me Juliet. What's wrong with Mom or Mother?"

"Female Parental Unit? XX Chromosomal Donor?" I offer.

Mom takes my spoon and swallows a bite. She gives me a thumbs-up and smiles, but her eyes water, and she stands up and spits the gruel into the trash. She puts the trash back under the sink, opens the cabinet, and plops a box of Crunch Berries cereal on the table.

"You're right, that's terrible."

"Juliet, you're many wonderful things, but a cook isn't one of them." She laughs.

"Milk, please?"

Mom nods and pulls the milk from the fridge. "Well, Fruit of My Loins, I did schedule the Girls! Do Work! rally on vocation day because promoting lifelong dedication to a man, no matter how spectacular his abilities, isn't appropriate career counseling."

She reaches her hand into the box and shoves pink berry nuggets into her mouth. "And besides, any man, even one who walks on water, can eventually leave you."

Mom points to the clock. "You're going to be late."

I grab a handful of cereal and put my bowl of gruel in the sink and make a sign of the cross in Mom's direction. "Lord, forgive the woman who made this congealed sin, for she knew not what she did."

Mom tries to snatch the dish towel off my head, but I duck, grab my book bag, and run outside just in time to catch the bus.

Despite the banners in the hall—"Listen to Your Heart Phone!" and "Hope He Calls!"—no one has heard God's call by fourth period, so the sisters order the entire junior class to the gym for mandatory hearing tests. The nurse is shining a tiny flashlight into Patty McCollough's ear when the PA chimes and announces my ride is waiting in the circle drive. Time to swap God weirdness for mother weirdness. When I was five, riding in the pencil-shaped van was thrilling, but at sixteen it's humiliating. I've put off getting my driver's license because there's no freedom in the open road when your car is a giant pencil on wheels, but such is life when your XX chromosomal donor owns the most successful pencil factory on the East Coast. The factory has been in our family for

generations, and Mom says Juliet Pencils is like Judaism: rich with tra-
dition and inherited through the mother. I like to remind her of other
matrilineal transfers: colorblindness, hemophilia, madness. All women
in the Rosenblum family are named Juliet because they will eventually helm the pencil factory that bears our name, but Mom named me
Frankie. People assume Frankie is short for Francesca, but it's not; it's
short for Franklin, as in Franklin Delano Roosevelt.

When I asked Mom why she didn't choose a more appropriate
name, something like Eleanor, she said, *Frankie, the First Lady? Aim
higher.*

Mom's secretary, Ron, drives me to the factory, and after we park
and I pick up a hard hat, I head straight to the break room, hoping there
are donuts. Juliet Pencils makes the pencils for Ding Dong Donuts:
they have a tiny hole in their barrel and a finish that looks like fudge
glaze. The break room is empty, but on the table is the telltale orange-
and-pink Ding Dong Donuts box. I throw my backpack on an empty
chair and open the box.

> *Frankie,*
> *Put down the donut. There are carrot sticks in the fridge.*
> *Mom*

I push the note aside and pick up a fudge-covered donut, and as the
crispy sugar dough relents, I address the empty chair across the table.
"Excellent carrot." I lick my fingers and pick up powdered-sugar bits
from the bottom of the box as Esther pokes her head into the room.
She plops in a chair and looks at the donut box.

"You ate the best ones."

"I left the cake one."

"A cake donut is neither cake, nor donut, because a donut without
icing is—"

"A pastry abomination?" I add.

"Good one, brainiac. Yes, a pastry abomination. I can't eat it anyhow. Icing makes my teeth wince. How's school?" she asks.

"The dumb leading the blind."

"That good?"

"We spent the day getting our hearing checked because none of us heard God's phone."

Esther holds her hand like a phone and laughs. She points to the yellow scarf sticking out of my backpack.

"Adventurers meeting tonight, Miss Cellaneous?"

Miss Cellaneous is Esther's nickname for me. Until I was old enough to stay by myself, the school bus dropped me off at the factory, and I'd hang out in Esther's lab, playing dress-up in her inventory shelves. No matter how bad the wig or how big the shoes, she would pull whatever pencil she was testing out of her mouth and hold it like a microphone and sing her version of the Miss America song, *Here she comes, Miss Cellaneous!* I would wave like a beauty queen, pretending the boxing glove or slop bucket was my bouquet and state sash.

"Yup. Meeting tonight. Best part of my day."

"Noah and Frankie camping in the woods, k-i-s-s-i-n-g." Esther winks and I roll my eyes.

Noah is my boyfriend. I guess. I mean he is, but we think those words are dumb. We don't say *boyfriend* or *girlfriend*, we just say Noah and Frankie. Noah is my Noah, blue eyes, messy brown hair, and a laugh that makes me laugh. I met him in Patriot Adventurers, and we were friends for a long time before we admitted that we liked each other. I didn't want to be a Patriot Adventurer. I wanted to be a Forest Nymph, but it's hard to convince a woman who runs a pencil empire to support an organization whose goal is selling cookies. Everyone in third grade was a Forest Nymph, and I liked the pictures in the brochure: girls sitting by a campfire, braiding each other's hair, although even at eight, I knew any girl who tried to braid my hair would need hot oil and a heavy hand. When I asked to join, Mom said learning to bake dooms you to a life of baking, but I think her real problem was with the sash.

"Do you know who wears sashes?" she asked.

I looked down at my shoes, which is what I do when I know I can't win. I can describe my shoes in numbing detail.

She continued, "Beauty queens and women in parades. Is that what you want? To be judged by men for your looks?"

"But, there won't be any men. It's Forest Nymphs," I said.

"No."

"But I'll learn about cookies and camping . . ."

"Cookies? Go to a bakery. Hell, own a bakery. Camping? You want to sleep outside?" She opened the sliding glass door. "There's the yard. Go ahead."

The next day she came into my room.

"You're right. I'll take you to a meeting."

After school we drove to the south side of town. The church basement smelled like mothballs and stale sugar cookies. A man looked up from his clipboard. "You want the church on the north side," he sighed.

My mom said, "I know where I am."

I looked at Mom, confused by the fight in her voice. She continued, "My daughter wants to learn to camp, but I don't want her to waste time selling cookies. It's demeaning to her gender."

The man put down his clipboard. "I don't care if she's a fish, she can't join the Patriot Adventurers. It's for boys and she's not a boy."

"That's discriminatory," Mom said.

"Sweetheart, unless your she is a he"—he tipped the clipboard my way—"*it* ain't joining."

"Why do you care that I'm a girl?" I asked.

Mom looked surprised, and the guy with the clipboard sighed again.

"Join Forest Nymphs and learn to sew. Learn things you'll need in life."

By the time we walked back to the car, I didn't know if I should be more mad at Mom for tricking me or more mad at the man who wouldn't let me join an organization I wasn't even sure I wanted to join. I sent a letter to a local chapter, but that didn't work. Mom sent a thousand-signature petition signed by everyone in the factory (Esther later told me that everyone thought they were signing up for double-donut Tuesdays), but that didn't work. Mom called the mayor, and when that didn't work, I called the mayor, and when that didn't work, she called the governor, and when that didn't work, I called the governor, and that's what worked.

Esther looks at the clock. "Time for TV."

I shove another donut in my mouth while Esther motions for me to tuck in my shirt and brushes powdered-sugar crumbs from my navy school blazer. Mom told me I probably wouldn't have to say anything during the interview, but just in case she made me practice the phrase *the joy of feminine self-sufficiency!* It took a long time before I could say it without laughing.

"Get out there and show the world the joy of self-sufficiency." Esther grins.

"See? You can't say it without laughing either."

I lean against the heavy door, the only thing separating me from fake smiling for live television.

Esther goads, "C'mon, say it!"

I plant my feet and push my back into the door bar. The door opens, filling the break room with the buzz and hum of heavy machinery. I lean forward, tip my hard hat to Esther, and shout, "The joy of feminine self-sufficiency!"

My nun impression might have been crap, but at least my last words to Esther were right on because nothing beats a hat tip and a joke about jerking off.

ESTHER

I hope my job security is in better shape than my lab coat.

To erase the previous client and prepare myself for the next, I have to recalibrate my bite by clenching around the edge of a ream of paper. It normally takes about five minutes, but I've been gnawing on this stack for more than twenty. I keep sneezing, and the order bell keeps ringing, and my nose keeps dripping, and I'm ready to shove paper up my nose and hurl the rest of the stack at that stupid dinging bell. I move my jaw, hoping to find the one spit-free spot, but instead I sneeze, and sheets of paper scatter across my desk and spill onto the floor. I peel off the piece that's stuck to my face and tilt my head to stop my nose from running. No wonder the bell won't stop: the large overhead feeder arteries are totally jammed. New clusters of pencils speed through the tubes and crash into the logjam of stuck pencils. Nothing can pass, and everything is banging into everything else at 60 mph, and splintering graphite fogs the transparent tubes. The only way to relieve the increasing pressure is to open a delivery chute on the factory floor, but if someone does that, pencils will torpedo across the factory and pummel the workers, guests, and the TV crew here for the Girls! Do Work! rally. I check the TV crew's schedule. They're on the floor now.

I wonder if raising my delivery hatch could jostle something loose. I pull, but the hatch won't open because it's pressure sealed. I smack the side of the tube but nothing budges. I smack harder. Nothing. I lean back, and with the heel of Dr. Chevalier's pump I kick the tube, and the latch pops and hisses, and pencils rush down out of the tube and skitter across the floor. The bell stops.

I do a small victory twirl, ignore my lab coat in the trash, and walk toward the back of my office to get a broom. I rub my jaw. See, guys? Just a bit of sweeping and I will reclaim this day. As I reach for the broom, the floor shakes and something loud rumbles over my head. I look up.

Glass bursts, and the rest of the backed-up pencils crash on the ceiling. The ceiling can't bear that much pressure or weight. It starts cracking, and the fissures race across faster than I can follow them. Oh no. I yank a Styrofoam cooler from the inventory shelf and run just as the ceiling hurls itself onto the floor. I dive behind the shelves and shove the cooler on my head. Glass stabs the back of my knees, pencils needle my spine and pierce my cooler helmet. My teeth clench so hard that my eye twitches. I can't see, and all I hear are booms and shattering glass. I'm afraid if I move I'll roll over onto glass, but my teeth feel like they are going to crack in half, so I lift the cooler just enough to pull out a pencil that's stuck in the side and shove it in my mouth. From inside the cooler, I push out a few pencils and use their punctures as peepholes.

When the plummeting glass slows, I carefully stand and pull the cooler off my head. My legs shake and my nylons are shredded and bloody. My office is ruined, a pencil Gettysburg. Everything on my inventory shelves, even my wig stands, are porcupined. I step over piles of glass and pencils and ceiling, trying to reach the door and get out.

The corridor leading to the factory floor is smoky, and I can barely see. My ears ring and my eyes throb, and I hold my shirtsleeve over my mouth, but my throat fills with silt anyway. I palm the walls until I find the door to the factory floor. I lean in and open it. Another explosion. Screams. The graphite foreman stumbles toward me. He yanks a pencil from his cheek and falls on the floor. I yell, "Help!" and powder rushes my throat, caking my lungs. I lean over and gag. Someone pulls me to the floor, the only sliver of clean air.

The light over the graphite vat flashes red. Emergency sirens wail. Across the factory floor Juliet drops to her knees. She slumps over a body and screams.

RUTH

Inside the camera obscura, fire defies gravity; flames hang from the ceiling, their forked and blazing tongues shouting across the walls. Chunks of the factory plummet, clouds of ash and debris float across the ceiling. Exterior smoke fogs the lens, funneling the room in gray and haze. I uselessly wave my arms, trying to clear the smothering whorls.

Ambulances speed into the parking lot, red-and-blue lights flash across the floor. Fire trucks and police cars, caution tape unspools and cordons. More firemen and more water, torrents splash up the walls and pool on the ceiling, disobeying physics and ignoring reason.

Paramedics rush out, carrying a body on a stretcher. In the smoke, I can't tell who it is, and then the wind shifts. Juliet runs out of the building, her mouth stalled in a scream. I can't hear her, but that doesn't matter, I know that look. A limp arm slumps over the edge of the stretcher. Juliet reaches for it, but the paramedics push the stretcher into the ambulance before she can touch it. She scrambles into the back, and the paramedics slam the door. I hold my palm over the ambulance and follow it across the wall until it slips out of view. Godspeed.

Smoke pours from the factory windows. The neon pencil disappears. Water flings across the camera obscura walls until the wind shifts again. I see Sam running across the street, cameras swinging from his neck. He stops and turns around to photograph the factory, then rushes toward me, waving his arms until he's out of lens range.

I run to the front of the store as the bell on the front door jingles, and before I can see him, I smell him, acrid oil and charred walls. He leans against the counter, his big body splayed like a busted hinge. His hands are on his knees and he is heaving, struggling to unyoke from carbon's drag. I grasp the side of his photo vest and pull him up, then grab a mug and fill it with water.

"Here. Drink."

He puts the mug on the counter, and I reach to refill it, but his fingers wrap around mine. My husband, Max, and I never had children, so I'm free to have as many sons and daughters as I want, and I consider Sam one of them. I squeeze his hand, but I don't say anything because words are useless for people like us, people who speak in images. Besides, there are no words that can make the seen unseen. Smoke blows into the store parking lot, and Sam holds my hand harder. I want to wrap my arms around him, I want to worry and weep, but my job is to help him solidify, not fall apart.

I've known Sam for decades, ever since he was a kid with *National Geographic* dreams. When he asked for photography lessons, I said yes even though it was something I'd never done and haven't done since. He was a darkroom hazard, all spindle limbs and dinner-plate hands knocking over bottles of chemicals and dropping film, but now his images are published all over the country. I'm not his mother, but I'm just as proud. I pry my fingers free and touch the top of his head—thick wads of graphite and plaster.

Sam wears multiple cameras around his neck because it's faster to have two cameras at the ready than to switch lenses in the middle of a shoot. I lift two of them from his neck and feel the bottoms for the buttons that release the film. I find them and then turn each camera's rewind crank. Sam's motto is, If the picture isn't good enough, he wasn't close enough, but putting yourself in the middle of the action, instead of using a telephoto lens to make the action come to you, is the hardest way to frame the world. His labored breathing and the burned smell roiling off him are unnecessary proof. I already knew he stood in the middle of calamity and calculated shutter speed and aperture. He didn't think about being in danger, he just thought about the shot. He witnesses the worst days of people's lives, and despite his motto and despite his training, heaviness accumulates in his core, imperceptible but undeniable, like the photons that crash into our skin every day.

The film's tension releases and I remove a roll of film from each camera. Sam reaches into his bag, pulls out six more rolls of exposed film, and puts them on the counter.

"Push everything two stops. I'm going to the hospital," he says.

"Juliet won't like that,"

"Call a courier, I gotta make tonight's deadline."

I put six fresh rolls of film on the counter.

"Sam?"

He loads his cameras and puts the remaining film in the pockets of his photo vest.

Sam has sat at my kitchen table and described ten-car pile-ups and wheat reaper dismemberments with cold-beer swagger, but he's never said things were bad. He gathers his gear and squeezes my hand once more, leaning down so I can kiss his cheek.

"That bad?" I ask.

He slings the cameras around his neck.

"That bad," he says.

"Stay safe. Look good," I say, because that's what we say to each other.

"Always," he says.

The bell on the door jingles as Sam walks out.

I flip the sign from **Open** to **Developing Memories!** and take Sam's film to the darkroom where I will process and make visible what I do not want to see.

ESTHER

Firemen evacuate the factory. We walk into the sun and squint, some people smoke, some people cry, and everyone wants to help, but we're not firefighters or medics, so we cough and wheeze and stand in the parking lot with our bloody palms and ripped, sooty uniforms. I lean over and pull a splinter from the roof of my mouth.

I drive home with the car windows down, but the wind doesn't block the ringing in my ears. A school bus turns in front of me, and after a few streets, it stops and a group of kids get off. The bus pulls back into traffic, and as I shift into first, a red water balloon smacks my windshield, and water sloshes on the passenger seat. The kids point and laugh. I turn on my wipers, but they're useless. The rest of my way home the balloon sticks to the middle of the windshield. I pull into my apartment building's parking lot and leave the balloon where it is. I pass the mailboxes and walk up the stairs to my fifth-floor apartment, holding my keys with both hands. I drop them twice before I manage to open my door.

Same shag carpet, same brown couch, same orange cushions, same afghan. How is everything the same when nothing is the same? My purse slumps off my arm, and I drop my keys near the key dish, but they fall off the table and hit the floor. My skin smells like burned wood. I've got to get out of these clothes. I unbutton Dr. Chevalier's blouse and unzip and step out of my skirt and slip. Pulverized graphite bracelets my wrists and collars my throat. I unroll the waist of my pantyhose. Dried blood pastes the hose to my shins. I tug and rip the nylon, and bits of wood fall on my shoes, and clouds of ash puff out of the weave. I unhook my bra and lean forward. Pencil shards fall on the carpet without the decency of making a sound, so thin they won't declare themselves yet so sneaky they just closed an entire factory and stabbed Miss Cellaneous.

And that's when I finally let myself cry.

I scrub and lather, rinse and repeat, but it's no use. Underneath green shampoo and marbled soap, I'm smoke and ash. The clogged water refuses to drain even after I scoop the woody bits out of the shower. I floss slivers from my gums and lean over the sink and open-mouth bleed. The bathroom fills with steam, as if I brought the accident home with me. I grab the door and fan cool air in from the hall. I rinse the blood out of the sink with my palm, turban my hair, tighten my robe, and pad into the kitchen. I take a glass from the dish drainer and open the high cabinet over the fridge. I grab the bottle by the neck, and we slump on the couch. The glass is pointless.

The first swig is long, and it's all for me. The second is for my teeth. I tilt my head from side to side and rummy waves crest my molar decks and seep underneath my gums, a ship tossing on rough seas. I pull the afghan down from the back of the couch and balance the rum on my chest. The bottle rises and falls with my breath. My hair smells like smoke, so I part my lips and blow, until all I smell is rum.

Teeth remember everything. Every popcorn kernel, mouth-torn strip of tape, gnawed cuticle, rubbery brisket, lover's ear, and impromptu candy corn fangs. When I'm really anxious, I try to calm my teeth by thinking about my childhood, the yeasty tang of my father's loafers, the solid comfort of wooden crib spindles and vacuum cleaner hoses. Teeth don't sleep but they do need regular exercise, and while taco shells and Slim Jims are enough to keep most teeth in shape, my teeth aren't most teeth. Without rigorous conditioning their anxiety erupts.

I'll be okay for a day or two, maybe even three, but after that? How long does it take to rebuild a building? How fast can walls be built and machines repaired? A gulp of rum and another and another, moving my head up and down, a physical yes when all I feel is no. At the beginning of the day, I joked with Frankie and smelled like Dr. Chevalier's perfume. Now Frankie is in the hospital, and I smell like burned logs.

Another swallow and I pull the afghan over my head.

RUTH

I measure chemicals, adjust the hands of the glow-in-the-dark timer, turn off the white light, and turn on the red safelight. I pour developer into a stainless steel tank and stand in thick redness, inverting and agitating the film. Film development is conjuration cloaked in highlight and shadow. In a flurry of light seeking light, the first chemical, developer, transforms film's trapped photons into crystalline images. It's the simplest of the processing stages because brightness is indiscriminate, brightness is easy, but shadows are slippery, they hollow out the negative. At the end of the developing process, light clumps and clings to the film but shadows refuse to bond. They slip off the film and tumble into the drain with the used chemistry. You can't taste them, and you won't see them, but they are there, in every swallow. Turn on the tap, fill a glass, and take a sip. Those shadows will slip down your throat, flooding your internal world.

Once the film is fixed, it's safe to turn on the white light. I pull the negatives from the tank, wash them, and hang them in the drying cabinet. I call the courier and schedule a pickup. When the dryer bell rings, I lay the negatives on the light table and look through my loupe at tragedy, elegantly framed. Clouds of smoke and water stopped midflow, defying time and sight as only photography can. The negatives are perfect, and the negatives are terrible.

Nothing is more important than how a person looks; I don't mean how they appear, I mean how they see the world. Most people look at photographs and reminisce, laughing about good times and ridiculous hairdos; they focus on the picture's subject and don't care how the picture was made, because when the flash pops and the shutter slams, normal people smile and say, *Cheese!* But, when Sam and I look at photographs, we don't only think about the subject, we think about the consequences of trapping the sun in a lighttight box. We think about stopping the spinning world and, in an instant, transforming the full present now into the flat, frozen past. What was once inherently fleeting is now irrevocably stopped. Infinity within a finite 35 mm rectangle, because looking at a photograph is being in two places at once: instant death and cheap immortality.

When the courier arrives, he wants to talk about the accident, but I shoo him out the door because as long as I can stay in the darkroom, I won't see the moonrise, and as long as it stays today, it can't be tomorrow because tomorrow I will have to sell film and calibrate my color printers, tomorrow I will have to open the cash register, taking dollars and returning nickels. *Yes, it's terrible. Yes, a blood drive. Yes, casseroles, and yes, hospital visits.*

For the rest of the night, I keep myself busy processing film and sliding glossy prints into Vixen envelopes. On the bottom of the envelopes is a disclaimer: *Prints unclaimed after 60 days will be destroyed.* People forget to pick up their film, but I don't think that forgetting to pick up your film means forgetting what you photographed, because photographing anything means believing something is worth remembering. Each of those thirty-six exposures is a choice. Some choices are quick, one five-hundredth of a second. Other choices require hours, days, or even years of waiting for the right moment: a birth, a wedding, an eclipse. Pretending to forget isn't the same thing as actually forgetting. I pretend to forget that Tuesdays exist, but something always comes between Monday and Wednesday.

My husband, Max, died on a Tuesday. That morning he'd brought me coffee in bed, one thing led to another, and I was late for work, again. Just another Tuesday in what I assumed would be a long chain of Tuesdays. I wasn't twenty when I fell in love; I was more than twice that, replete with a middle-aged body and the middle-aged realization that fighting about a sink full of dirty dishes was good because it meant I'd managed to create a real life, messy and extraordinary, with someone else. Success on my own was easy. I started a business and it thrived, but a business isn't a life, and life without a beloved is just killing time.

When the phone rang that Tuesday, I was in the darkroom calibrating the color printer, and I answered like I always did, *Vixen Photo, how can I help you look better?* The receiver slipped from my hand, and for the first time in a decade, I turned on the light without thinking and in a split second ruined a thousand dollars' worth of film. It was late afternoon; I laid on the horn and sped through red lights. The sun was setting. I've hated sunsets ever since. By the time I reached the hospital, he was dead but I didn't know, and so I parked the car with shaky hands and uxorial hope. The admitting clerk would only tell me that there had been an accident: *The patient is still in surgery.* I tried to bribe her with free film, but it didn't work. So I cried, but that didn't work either. And then I yelled. She shook her head and said, *I'm sorry, there are rules.* I paced and waited, blank stares and dry heaves, bargaining with a god I'd ignored. I will kiss him more. I will stop caring about wet towels on the floor. Why did I ever care about wet towels on the floor? When a nurse finally called my name, she looked at her clipboard and then at her shoes, and I knew the news wouldn't be good. Broken legs? Heart attack? Stroke? He loved butter. Why didn't I insist on margarine? I will insist on margarine. Please. The nurse gestured toward a surgeon still in his scrubs. *This is Ruth, the wife.* The surgeon touched my shoulder. He said, *I'm sorry.* I ran to the bathroom and vomited and then gripped the sink so I wouldn't fall as I rinsed my mouth. The surgeon said it was a car accident. Max was conscious at the scene, but his consciousness didn't last. I looked at my legs and commanded they stand, but they didn't obey.

I gathered my limbs, and then I collected what the hospital called Mr. Stanhope's belongings. One gold wristwatch, one brown shoe, and a head of lettuce, because we'd talked earlier in the day about eating salad for dinner. I asked about his wedding ring, but the young man who held the bag in front of me shook his head and said, *Sometimes in accidents things get lost.* So I walked to my car and stood in the parking lot with the best half of my life stuffed in a plastic bag.

I couldn't throw away the lettuce. Of all the green heads he'd selected this one, he'd put it in his cart, waited in line, chatted with the cashier, carried the bag to his car. He'd probably put it on the front seat and then pulled out of the parking lot without a second thought because that's what life is: choosing lettuce and pulling out of parking spaces until you're dead. When I asked for his clothes, they said, *We had to cut them off.* Was he singing with the radio? When the EMTs slid him into the ambulance, did he think about me? Was he in pain? Did he wish I were there? The lettuce decomposed into mephitic sludge, and for the next year I refused salads and for the most part pretended the refrigerator didn't exist. I adjusted to black coffee; I ate dry toast. When the new fridge arrived, the delivery guy inspected the old one and said, *There's nothing wrong with this.* I nearly threw my dry toast and black coffee in his face. A few months after the accident, the insurance company sent a typewritten letter clearing Max of any culpability. They suspected he had swerved to avoid hitting something, perhaps a house cat or maybe a person, but they couldn't confirm any details, so the case was resolved, a check was enclosed, and just like that, I was a widow.

FRANKIE

I open my eyes. There's a tube in my arm. Blood flows out of it and into a vial. I try to open my mouth, but before sound can come out, a man presses his hand to my forehead. "I'm Nurse Paul. Don't talk."

RUTH

"Ruth. Ruth, wake up."

I roll over and open my eyes, a disorienting fact in a darkroom. I pat the top of my head for my glasses, but I don't feel them.

Sam hands my glasses to me and I put them on, and the darkness sharpens. I tuck my hair behind my ears and sit up. Even in the red light Sam looks a bit green.

"Can I stop it?"

I make room for him on the couch, but he paces, his hands rabbiting from pocket to pocket in his photo vest.

"Stop what?"

"I need to take it back," he says.

"Take back what? Sam, what time is it?"

Sam peels the tape off the digital clock.

"Three a.m. I need to turn on the light. Can I turn on the light? Everything away?"

"Yeah, all good."

Sam turns on the white light and pulls a newspaper out of his shoulder bag and spreads it across the light table. The front-page photographs show factory workers knee-deep in shattered pencils, ashen horror spread across their faces.

I know these images because I processed the negatives, but there's something dire about seeing them in print. The flatness of blood, the

heaviness of smoke, all the frenzy—stilled and framed. Flying projec-
tiles, workers with their hands on their heads, a mother slumped in
shock. Sam scratches his stubble.

He reaches in his bag and pulls out another newspaper, the national
one. Workers with streaky gray faces cling to each other; some are crying and some point at exploded machinery. Juliet's mouth is stalled
midscream, and her blouse is marred by dark smears as Frankie's body
is loaded into the ambulance. The *Lead Sentinel* only prints in color
on Saturdays, so for everyone looking at the local paper, the blood is
dark gray, and somehow that looks worse. There's no oxygen, it's deader
than dead.

Sam pushes his fingers into the paper so hard that the ink smears.

"Sam, you did your job."

"That image of Juliet. The editor overruled me. I want to take it
back."

I lean forward and put my hand on his.

"People shouldn't see this; no one needs to see that kid with a pencil
stuck in her throat."

"Honey, it's been printed."

"The trucks are out now. I've got to do something. Maybe if we
hurry, we can . . ."

I've got that feeling again, like someone replaced my bones with
wet sand. I don't understand why the lack of early-life tiredness hurls
itself forward and dumps into late middle age. I don't say yes but I can't
say no.

The darkroom door is a black cylinder that spins 180 degrees,
preventing outside light from leaking inside, because the very thing
that film needs is also what will destroy it. When Sam first learned
to develop film, he thought the darkroom door looked like a portal
to another world, like something from a science fiction movie, and
tonight I hope he is right. Sam steps into the spinning door, and when

the opening returns to me, I hope there's a parallel world because this one feels like it's turning the wrong way.

Sam waits by the counter.

"The van?" Sam asks.

"Keys are on the hook by the register."

"You'll need to drive."

I figure it's better to not ask, so I grab the keys and my purse, and we pull out of the Vixen parking lot. The stoplight by the pencil factory is red. I don't want to look at the white trails of smoke, an unfortunate streak of contrast in the nighttime blackness, so I look both ways and then go through the light.

"Thanks," Sam says.

"Is this a long trip or a short trip?" I ask.

"Short trip, but a long time."

A few blocks ahead, a *Lead Sentinel* delivery truck turns in front of us.

"Pull over and turn off the lights."

I pull to the curb, and Sam slides down in his seat. The newspaper truck slows but doesn't stop, and a man leans out of the back and throws three bundles of the morning editions on the sidewalk.

Sam tugs my sleeve. "Ruthie, slide down, don't let them see you."

"Sam, we're not going to—"

"Yeah, we are."

"Sweetie, we can't keep up. We're just one van and, what, there are dozens of trucks?"

"There are ten trucks."

The truck returns to the lane and continues.

"You can get up now."

Sam rises in his seat and points to the bundled newspapers on the sidewalk. "Pull up." He steps into the back of the van, and as I drive near the curb, he slides open the van door, leans out, and grabs the papers by their twine and throws them back into the van before I've even shifted into park. I turn around and look at him, three bundles of newspapers in the huge cargo space.

"I'll stay back here. It'll be easier."

We follow the newspaper truck at a distance, and a few blocks up we turn left, and Sam grabs three more bundles.

After an hour, we have a system. We stop for gas, and I rest my head against the van and listen to the pump numbers click and flip. I go into the mini-mart and pour a cup of coffee, pay with a large bill, and request my change in quarters. The *Sentinel* truck arrived at the gas station before we did. Sam empties the rack and pays for all the papers. The cashier doesn't recognize Sam, the reality of being a photographer. Sam frames the world, yet remains invisible.

As I pull out of the gas station, papers scatter across the back of the van. I pass my coffee to Sam, and he takes a long sip, then rolls down the window and pushes in the cigarette lighter. He passes the coffee back to me. I take another sip and dump the rest out the window. The lighter pops. Sam lights his cigarette and inhales. I pass the empty cup and point to the rolls of quarters in the center console. He ashes out the window and unwraps the quarters and dumps them into the large cup.

When we pass a newspaper rack, Sam says, "Here," and takes quarters from the cup. I pull over, and Sam opens the box and grabs every paper and slings them into the van. After we empty all the boxes downtown, we drive through all of Lead's neighborhoods. Up and down streets, across lanes, and around cul-de-sacs, if there's a newspaper on a front lawn or a porch step, Sam steals it. A paperboy, in reverse.

As the sun rises, we're exiting the lobby of an apartment building, our arms full of bad news. The radio has been off all night, but as we leave the parking lot, I turn it on. Sam cycles through the dial as I drive toward the Vixen, where we started. Every station is giving detailed reports about the accident. Sam turns off the radio.

"Breakfast?" I ask.

"I can't. Got to get back to the paper and make up some reason I don't have photos from the hospital."

I pull into the Vixen parking lot, and Sam steps out of the van.

"What the hell am I supposed to do with all of these?" I ask.

"Storage space?"

I nod and watch Sam pull out of the parking lot.

I didn't stand in the pencil factory and meter the light. I didn't think about the compositional rule of thirds or calculate the relationship between aperture and shutter speed. I didn't activate my camera's motor drive so I could shoot without stopping, and I didn't experience the synergy of my camera as an extension of myself. I wasn't there, but I made the images possible, and I wish I hadn't. I sold the film, and I developed the negatives, and those negatives were transferred onto metal plates that were inked and then printed onto large rolls of newsprint, and that newsprint was cut, sorted, and tied into bundles, and loaded onto trucks, and delivered across town, flung on front porches and stuffed into curbside boxes. It's a mechanized, streamlined process that happens every day and every night. I made the images possible, and something seen can't be unseen. There is no visual apology. I can't unload the camera; I can't rewind the film. And since I can't take it back, since I can't alter the past, I have to make the future look better. I will calibrate my printers better than I ever have. No more sirens and no more flashing lights and no more blood. Reds will be strawberries, not fire. White will be eggs and magnolias, not smoke. Blues will be a dive under sunlit water: go ahead, open your eyes, and look; I promise it won't sting.

ESTHER

Someone stole my newspaper.

While the television warms up, I scoop coffee into the percolator and watch the liquid bump against the glass nob. Anchorman Chuck says, "catastrophic accident" and "economic impact," and then cuts to a commercial. A woman wearing a white blouse tucked into white pants runs through a field of daisies and smiles; a male voice-over says, "You'll feel secure!" No one wears white pants on their period, dumbass. The commercial ends, and the Channel Six special news bulletin chimes. Chuck looks into the camera. "Breaking news bulletin. The Juliet Pencils factory will be closed for at least thirty days."

I swallow hard, hoping to drown out Chuck's voice. Too late. My teeth heard him. They clench, and coffee dribbles down my chin. I place my mug on the table. Calm mind, calm mouth, Esther. That's what the dentist suggested. Calm mind, calm mouth. I can wear white pants on my period. I can run through fields of daisies. I grab the channel knob. Breathe in; I am filled with daisy freedom. Breathe out; I am white-pants confident. Chuck repeats the news. I hold my jaw and try to turn the knob with my elbows. ". . . catastrophic economic impact," next channel, ". . . closed for more than a month . . . ," the last channel, ". . . large percentage of the town is suddenly unemployed." I press my back against the television, static charges my frizzy hair. I massage my gums with my fingers. Field of daisies. Smell the daisies. You'll be fine. Wait, daisies don't really smell. Do daisies smell? Spit drips from my fingers. Hang on, guys. I'll think of something. I scoot away from the TV and lay my cheek on the coffee table. Steam rises from my mug. The last time I didn't work for longer than a three-day weekend, I ended up with a cracked molar and a bruised jaw. I used to keep a spare box of pencils at home for downtime relief, but my dentist urged me to cultivate a better work/life balance, so now all my pencils are at work, in a building the fire chief has declared unsafe. I pull a corner of the afghan off the couch and wipe my drool. I try to sip, but my jaw clenches, and I spill burning coffee down my bare legs. Thirty days, one day for each tooth.

RUTH

I don't think of it as stealing. Stealing is taking something that doesn't belong to you, but time belongs to no one, which means time belongs to everyone, and photographs are nothing but time. One moment, selected, flattened, and preserved from a continuous stream that, for shorthand's sake, people call life.

Since 1839 when photography was invented, billions of people have taken billions of pictures. Across every continent and in every country: camera, カメラ, *aparat fotograficzny*, and 相機. Billions of seconds have been removed from the stream of time, and no one ever replaces what they take. Kids in footed pajamas on Christmas morning or an elephant's trunk curled around a peanut, the image is irrelevant. All that matters are the accumulated seconds yanked from the stream of time. Seconds become minutes and minutes become hours and hours become days and days become months, school years, summers, cakes baked without reason, sex in the middle of the afternoon: it's a lifetime. One more touch, one more thunderstorm, one more winter. With enough time, lungs expand and blood circulates. I can roll over and spread my legs, more, yes, there. Again. Although the disclaimer on the Vixen envelope says that unclaimed prints will be destroyed, it's a lie. After Max died, I started saving all the unclaimed prints.

Determining the amount of time trapped in a photograph isn't difficult. Technical choices affect a photograph's appearance, so any trained photographer can look at an image and estimate what shutter speed and aperture were used; and while it's not an exact science, it's close enough. When the boxes of unclaimed images still fit in my guest room, I spent most nights at the dining room table sorting them. I drank Scotch; I was jealous. Sometimes I knew the people or recognized the locations, but I never understood the reasons for pretending something once worth preserving no longer mattered. After a few months, when a customer ordered thirty-six prints, I'd print more, and keep the extras, and soon enough the guest room and dining table weren't enough space, so I rented a storage unit under the name Jackie Daguerre. Inside that space, I pushpinned and stapled snapshots on the walls until they were covered, five layers deep, in other people's memories. Subject matter and composition were irrelevant. I didn't care if the picture was a cooing baby or an out-of-focus bundle of sticks; I just wanted to surround myself with rectangles of reclaimed time.

I kept one of Max's shirts at the storage unit. Soft blue cotton, ten buttons, and a discreet navy *MS* monogrammed on the pale-blue cuffs. He wore it one evening, maybe it was our fifth date? It's difficult to remember because after our fourth my sense of time was unreliable: one evening with him was weeks of evenings with other men. Max was a concentrate and the others mere dilutions. I remember him wearing it in the terrine of September, layers of pine needles and flambéed oak leaves. The season of approaching surrender. Our plan was a picnic by the lake, and we stopped at the grocery store to pick up a roasted chicken. My contribution was dessert: fresh cherries bundled in a crisp dish towel. I was going to knot their stems with my tongue and line them up on his thigh. We pushed our shopping cart toward the deli, and I pretended to care about roasted chickens, but all I actually cared about was standing close enough to feel the heat radiating from his chest and arms. The small market was crowded; women with arthritic hands knocked on the deli glass, requesting a quarter pound of Lorraine swiss, *thinly sliced.*

Max brushed his hand against mine and reached for a paper number, his shirt tightening across his shoulders. I leaned my elbows on the cart handle and stared at him, a gift disguised as a man. Max was patient; he smiled and passed paper-wrapped bundles to the elderly women. When our order was ready, he reached for the packet, and his unbuttoned cuff fell open, exposing his wrist, an innocuous flash, but at that point all his skin was cock skin—magnetic and transformative. He walked toward the cart and smiled, and I thought to myself: He's a luminous creature. He glowed; he made no sense, a giraffe in the toothpaste aisle, and yet somehow he—we—made the most sense, a glorious extravagance in a workaday world. It took me a long time to use the word love. It seemed too banal to describe what was happening. People love pizza, people love baseball, but what is the word when space dissolves and time slows and you see beyond monogrammed cuffs, beyond tanned wrists, through sinew and tendon, into the viscous conduit of explosive stardust origin? Is that love? What word explains that I see a candescent man while everyone else sees a guy holding a cooked chicken, walking past canned peas and toilet cleaner? Certainly that needs more than four letters. Max placed the chicken in the cart and traced the tiny peaks and valleys of my knuckles.

You okay? You look far away.

I'm here, I said. *I'm right here.*

He slipped his hand around my waist and pulled me close.

Back then I was naive enough to believe I controlled my material body, but now I know how easy it is to dematerialize without warning, without will. We skipped the picnic and drove to his house. The bed was too far, but the couch was right there, and as he started to unbutton his shirt, I spread his cuff and pulled his wrist between my thighs.

Ten buttons. Ten thumb-size planets—to touch them is to time travel. I slip the shirt on backward, sliding my arms where his used to be, a pale substitute for an embrace. As I lie on the couch, the buttons press into my vertebrae, and I remember all the times I unbuttoned this shirt, and I remember the times he undressed me while he wore this shirt. I remember the bottles of wine and the all-afternoon lazy sex that started when he stood behind me as I chopped carrots for stew and ended with both of us spent and laughing, trying to squeeze together on the living room couch. We ordered takeout because the stew burned. Ten buttons, but countless nights and weekends, a life, a universe. It wasn't his best shirt or his most expensive, but those sleeves transport me to the moment when our life began, to afternoons that unfurled like months, to when I first understood that love is gravity's reprieve, because when I fell in love I didn't fall down, I fell up—finally understanding my capacity for ascension.

The first time Max's favorite song came on the radio, I was driving to work. My hands were on the steering wheel, but I was in bed with him as he slipped his hands underneath my shoulders and moved them up to cradle the weight of my head. He liked to tease me that way. Only when I surrendered the full weight of my head would he brush his lips against mine and descend, kissing my clavicle's ridge, inner elbow, and junction of thigh, pelvis, and hip. I didn't see the blue car, not until I slammed into the back of it. There are no cars in bed, there is only me and Max. The policeman rapped his knuckles on the window. *Step out of the vehicle.* He opened the door and pried my hands off the wheel. *Are you okay?* I shook my head. He unbuckled my seatbelt. *Do you know where you are?* I shook my head again. I was entwined with a man and wrapped in sheets, and now I'm in the middle of the road, taillight shards and bumper chunks at my feet.

Friends offered to drive me everywhere. They interpreted my accident as anxiety or fear of driving, but it was the opposite: all I wanted to do was drive. I drove for made-up reasons and distended to-do lists: shampoo at one store and conditioner at another across town, and no matter where I was, before I drove home, I always drove to that grocery store. I didn't buy anything; I didn't even leave the car. I just looped the parking lot and exited by turning left, hoping to meet the same fate he had. I didn't use my signal, but it didn't matter: cars kept missing me and I kept missing him. I wondered if I was doing it wrong, so I varied my attempts: I turned faster and fiddled with the radio, but nothing worked because details are insignificant in the face of such a keelhaul, to fuck in the morning and be a widow by sunset. I tried a support group, a bunch of other widows in a church basement, drinking burned coffee from short Styrofoam cups. They discussed stages of grief and used words like *acceptance* and *moving on.* My folding chair scraped against the cement floor, and the group leader clucked her tongue and whispered, *Stage four: anger.* Grief isn't a stage. A stage is elevated, and after the actor performs, people applaud and want more. No one wants a grief encore. Grief is a shaft. Everyone stands above you, cultivating sad faces and tossing down useless sympathy cards that proffer nothing but paper cuts. The cards say stupid things like *I'm so sorry,* which actually means, *I'm so glad I'm not you.*

A year after Max's accident the police chief dropped off a large film order—something his secretary usually did but that day he said he wanted to thank me personally. Traffic fatalities were down by 19 percent. *People have been shaken by Max's accident,* he said.

I looked straight ahead. *Double prints or singles?*

After Max's death it was difficult to color balance customers' happiness when my own joy was cremated and shoved in an urn. Week after week, I smiled and handed customers glossy rectangles of their full lives, and I guess it took its toll because I started time traveling at work.

The first time it happened, I was with a customer who was in town to visit the St. Lucy shrine. It was a hot day, and as we talked about the weather, he unbuttoned his cuffs and rolled up his sleeves, exposing his tanned wrists. I held my breath as I rang up his order. I dropped his film into a bag, but it was too late. Max's arm curled around my waist, and my mouth filled with the taste of roast chicken and cherries. I ran to the back of the store, pressed my palms into my knees, and leaned over the toilet. I rinsed my mouth and looked in the mirror. How can I be alive if I keep disappearing, and how can he be dead if he keeps showing up? I returned to the register and made an unconvincing joke about a bad ham sandwich. He jingled the change in his pocket and asked, *Are you okay? What's* luminous creature? *Is that a type of film?*

My stomach tightened. I hadn't realized I'd said it out loud. *Yes, I'm thinking about manufacturing my own brand of film.* I waited until he pulled out of the parking lot, and then I flipped the door sign to **DEVELOPING MEMORIES!** and stayed in the darkroom for the rest of the day.

A negative is a piece of film embedded with trapped photons, and a shirt cuff is a band of fabric at the end of a sleeve, but the darkness of the negative and the tightness of the weave belie their real abilities. Shirt cuffs and film spools defy the logic of time and space. Before Max, I was alive and happy; I did what I wanted when I wanted. I built a business, I spent time with friends, I swam in the Great Lake. I didn't pine for baby carriages and matching towels, but when he came into my life, I unearthed my propensity for expansion, and once expanded, I couldn't deflate. The big bang can't be shoved back into its box. Max explained that everything from back then is our here and now.

You mean there's nothing new? I asked, rolling over in bed to face him.

He lifted his head from the pillow and smiled. *Nope, everything is made of the same exploded stardust.* He leaned over and dragged the sheet down my hips. It's a ridiculous system, using dead stars to make the coffee at the convenience store, and with all that pulverized star power, the coffee should taste better than burned socks, but I know that's not what he meant.

The world is tuned to single people trying to couple, and the world is deaf to couples that are suddenly single. It's impossible to buy one hamburger patty and one bun, but that's not why I stopped bringing hamburgers to the neighborhood barbecues. When I showed up, the husbands looked at their shoes, and the wives either clutched their husband's forearms as if widowhood were contagious, or they looked at me with envy because I was free from the domestic morass of clipping coupons and arguing about wet towels left on the floor. Colleagues presented Max's research paper, his doctor transferred his medical records from *active* to *deceased*, and his squash partner found someone else, but I didn't have a new partner, so I talked to my dead one. We chatted about the obvious and the inexplicable: *What's it like where you are? Is it cold? Do you miss me?* After my morning swim, I'd return to the car and drip on the seat, describing that morning's lake: *Choppy. I think I saw an old shoe.* Sometimes I threw my swimming goggles and towel on the passenger seat: *Hold these?* One morning I left Max's window rolled down and didn't notice there was a person in the car next to us. Max and I were chatty that morning. *Can you tell my stroke is improving? Yeah, you're right, the lake does smell fresh. What should we have for dinner?*

The woman from the other car popped her head in the passenger window, almost hitting Max in the face. *Honey? Are you talking to yourself? You got heatstroke or something?*

I leaned over and rolled up the window, but she just stood there, tapping her keys on the glass. As I pulled out of the parking lot, we laughed and decided on fresh corn for supper.

FRANKIE

I remember bits and pieces. Chuck, the Channel Six anchor, wore more makeup than Mom, and he kept calling me Francesca. The camera's light was so hot and bright it made my eyes water. Every time I shouted *Girls! Do Work!* I tried to not crack up, and by the time the cameraman yelled *Cut!* my uniform shirt was soaked. That's me, River Pits Rosenblum. Classic.

The last thing I remember is looking at the light above the graphite vat as it switched from green to flashing red. And now I'm here, hooked to machines with flashing lights. Paul is draining my blood again, but I must be in a different room because mine is the only bed. Paul loads vials filled with my insides into a wire rack, then presses a cotton ball on my inner elbow.

"Welcome back."

The cotton ball turns pale pink, then dark pink, then bright red as he unwraps a Band-Aid.

I'm bleeding.

I try to lift my arm, but I can't.

Paul glances at my arm. "You're bleeding."

I lift my arm off the sheet just enough to flip my wrist like a game show host who parts the curtain to reveal a new car or, with my recent luck, a washer-and-dryer combo.

"So you want to know more?" Paul asks.

I nod.

"The shah of Iran was overthrown, Great Britain has a lady prime minister, the lines for gas are five blocks long, and President Carter went fishing and had to fend off an attacking rabbit with his canoe paddle."

Paul picks up my chart, begins to write. I bang my fist on the bed, but the mattress swallows my frustration.

Paul looks up. "I know. Who knew rabbits could swim?" He returns the chart to the hook at the end of the bed and watches as I try to lift my head off the pillow. He sighs and grins. "Oh, you want to know about *you*. Well, you've had a tube down your throat. In the biz we call that intubation, but you can just call it good times. You had surgery to remove the pencil and all the other gunk that slammed into your throat, and you were in intensive care, but you're done with that, and now you're here with me."

I point to my wrist where a watch would be.

"It's Tuesday."

My eyes bug. Paul reaches over and flicks the IV bag. "Yeah. This stuff. Total time suck. You want me to help you sit up?"

I nod and point at my throat.

"Like someone shoved sandpaper down there?"

I shake my head. I'd kill for such silk.

"Then dumped a bag of cat litter on top?"

I nod.

Paul fluffs my pillows and opens the top drawer of the bedside table and pulls out a spiral notebook and a pencil. I recognize the pencil. The hospital is one of Mom's biggest customers.

"I thought this might help."

I try to smile, but it hurts to move my mouth, so I just give a thumbs-up.

"You're welcome, but I got you the notebook and pencil so you could *write*."

He overenunciates and mimics writing, as if I'm unfamiliar with the concept. I flip him the bird.

Paul is my favorite because he vampires my blood on the first try, and he's the only nurse who talks to me like a normal person. The other nurses confuse not speaking with not hearing. They shout when they come into the room, and they treat me like I'm six, not sixteen. All their sentences are singsong rhymes. Everyone asks the same two boring questions: *How is your pain?* and *How do you feel?*

The pain question is easy. My fingers are a built-in one-to-ten scale. But how do I feel? I answer that by pretending my right hand is a crank that raises the middle finger of my left hand. Crank on, fuck off. That's how I am.

Paul wheels his nurse cart toward the door. I open the notebook, scrawl a two-word directive, and bang my fist on the swing-out tray. I hold up the notebook.

Paul pivots and smiles. "Good job, sunshine. I knew you had it in you." He pushes the cart into the hallway, then pokes his head back in the doorway, and points to the notebook. "Survival tips scattered throughout."

I fan the notebook: *Beware the green Jell-O.*

ESTHER

I'm standing in the middle of the hardware store, mouth-testing pencil substitutes. Hammers are compelling but too heavy. Dowel rods seem promising until they reveal themselves as splintery disappointments. But toilet plungers are a total surprise, solid molar love with the added perk of stick-to-itiveness. I empty the shelf into my cart and ask the manager if he has more in the storeroom. He stares at my shopping cart and suggests antacids and consommé.

I'm okay.

This will be great. Free time. People like free time. I'm going to do all the stuff I never have time to do, stuff like cleaning and organizing, and handwashing, and when the factory opens in a month, my house will be tidy and my pantry will be unscrambled. Calm mouth, calm mind. I consolidate four jars of pickles into one jar of pickles and pick the dried jellied ring from the ketchup bottle. Calm mind, white pants. I alphabetize the contents of my freezer, carrots before peas, and Fudgsicles before potpies. Rearranging food makes me feel efficient and hungry. I follow a recipe that is too long and has too many ingredients, and by the time it comes out of the oven, I'm not hungry anymore, so I divide the food into containers to put in the freezer, but I can't figure out how to alphabetize them, so I ladle everything back into bowls and leave them on the counter.

In the bathroom I check expiration dates and build a barrier of baby powder and tampons to hide the antifungal cream because in my new world I'll run through daisy fields, not run to the pharmacy for rash ointment. I throw away bottles of conditioner that didn't keep their promises: there were flyaways. I wipe out my makeup bag and experiment with the eyeshadow palette I bought the last time I had a date. The saleswoman promised the colors would brighten my eyes and take years off my face, but it's been so long since I've used it that it smells like old-lady purse, and I can't remember which color is the highlighter and which is the contour and what I'm supposed to blend with the blending wand. When I finish, my eyes are bloodshot and puffy because I either overblended or undercontoured, but either way, I've added years to my face.

I dump an armload of sweaters, which have been in the bottom of my closet for months, into the sink. The bottle of wool wash says, *Don't wring, cold water only*, so I don't and I do. I swish-swirl until my eyeshadow is runny and my hands are pruny, and I remember why the sweaters were in the bottom of the closet in the first place. Handwashing is like No Flyaways! conditioner—bullshit promises and a total waste of time.

FRANKIE

Mom stands at the foot of the bed, beaming and surrounded by blooms.

"These are all for you," she says.

I roll my head across the pillow, and beyond her outstretched and bandaged arms are roses, nothing but roses—the Wonder Bread of blooming stuff. As a teenage XX I'm supposed to swoon over roses, but roses make me think of high school, and high school makes me think of nuns, and on the index of swoonable things, nuns are at the bottom, slightly above cat turds and those Crisco-thick scabs that won't come off no matter how much I pick them. My face hurts too much to smile, so at least I don't have to pretend to swoon over flowers that piss me off; but still, the sheer amount is impressive, even if I know the roses aren't really meant for me. They're for Mom, because when you employ most of the town, and your factory explodes, and your only kid gets stabbed in the throat, daisies just won't do. Daisies are a weed sent by people who already know the outcome but want to look like they care, but roses mean business. Roses are a *Sorry your factory's toast, and your daughter is temporarily mute!* type of flower, and that's why every flat surface of my room is covered with roses, and why the ceiling is crowded with helium balloons. At least the balloons are fun. If I'd known I'd get to sleep under a canopy of noble gas, I would have totally gotten into an industrial accident sooner.

Psych.

Not.

The air-conditioning kicks on and blows a **GET WELL SOON** into a rocket-shaped **SPEEDY RECOVERY**, transforming the ceiling into a slow-motion balloon derby. A floppy clown hovers over my bed and stares. It creeps me out. Clowns are the roses of the big top. No matter how much I tug the strings of surrounding balloons, I can't push floppy Bozo far enough to impale him on the spikes of the sprinkler. Operation Burst Bozo would be easier if I could get out of bed or stay awake, but I keep falling asleep, and even when I'm awake, it feels like I'm half-asleep. Sometimes I think I'm dreaming, but then a nurse jabs my arm, and I realize I'm awake, and a few times I thought I was awake, but then I realized I was dreaming about being in a hospital. It's confusing and annoying, like that time at Susan Heffernden's party when somebody passed around a bottle of gin, and everybody swigged and acted like they loved it, but all I could think was what shithead decided to stick a bush into a blender, and what bigger shithead decided to con the world into thinking frappéed bush tastes good?

When I wake up, Mom is sleeping in the brown recliner by the window. I try to wake her up by throwing wadded balls of notebook paper at her, but my aim is crap, and a small pile accumulates under the footrest. She looks like shit. Wet-finger-in-electrical-socket hair and eye bags like bug larvae. I want to hear what happened to the factory, and I want to know how Esther is, but I feel bad about waking Mom, and besides I don't even know how to wake her. She can't hear me; no one can hear me because my dumb mouth won't make any noise. It's just me, the beep-beep-beep machine, the sad-sack clown balloon, and the stupid roses, and they're the worst, they just stare at me, tight-lipped and boring.

The doctors touch my neck without asking. They call it palpitating. They poke me and pull up my gown. Their hands are like notebook paper pulled from a deep freezer. They scribble and huddle with each other. "Severe rupture. Extensive therapy." They talk in front of me, but they never talk to me. The medical students take notes and whisper, "Is this the one from the accident?"

I can hear you. I can hear all of you.

I used the notebook Paul gave me to write a list: *The Pros and Cons of Getting Stabbed in the Neck.* So far, it's short.

#1. Pro: No more speech class and no more chorus!

#2. Con: I can't say: asinine, antler, *or* cocksuckermotherfucker- douchebag, *my three favorite words.*

#3. Con: I don't know if I can say hello or good-bye or anything else to Noah when we finally talk on the phone.

The hospital is louder than I thought it would be: the hallway echoes with clicking doctors' loafers and swishing nurses' pantyhose, but it's not the noise that unnerves me, it's the silence. When I was at home, the phone would ring every night at ten thirty, and I'd run to answer it before Mom did, stretching the phone cord from the hallway into my bedroom and diving under the covers as Noah's voice cocooned in my ear. Some nights we talked about school or Patriot Adventurers, or we read to each other. Some nights I crammed all my vocabulary words into one long sentence, and Noah laughed so hard he'd lose his breath, but he kept repeating my name: *Frankie, Frankie, Frankie.* The two best sounds in the world are Noah laughing and Noah saying my name. It didn't matter that I was in my room and Noah was in his across town, because when we're on the phone, it feels like we're in the same space, a place that exists just for the two of us. The vocab word for that is *interstice*, and I realize this doesn't count for much since I've never left Ohio, but I know if I went to Jupiter, the first thing I'd want to do is call Noah and tell him about it. My bedroom is in the attic, so sometimes I dragged the phone out the window, lay on the roof, and described the sky. It didn't matter if I said the moon was plump like a Mentos or thin like a fingernail clipping, Noah said the same thing: *Let's spin through space.*

When I joined Patriot Adventurers, Noah was like the rest of the troop: he didn't look at me or talk to me. But all I did was stare at his dark wavy hair and hope he'd say words in my general direction. The troop wasn't mean; they just didn't understand why I was there. Fair enough, I didn't know why I was there either. The idea of not being allowed to join made me mad, so I worked hard to join, but then once I was in, I realized it was kind of weird to be the only girl. When the troop leader, George, introduced me, he said, *Boys, this is Frankie.* As if that was enough of an explanation. It wasn't, and the rest of the troop looked down at their sneakers instead of up at my face.

One time our troop was at the lake competing for the ichthyology badge, which as far as I could tell was heavy on the *ick* and light on the *ology. Plunge your blade into the anus, slice through the belly, and when you reach the top, chop off its head.* Those were George's instructions on gutting and scaling fish. When George said *anus*, everyone laughed and shoved their fists inside their trout and, voilà, instant fish puppets. Everyone assumed Noah would catch the most fish because he had the most badges, and everyone assumed I'd catch the fewest because I had no badges, and they were right. By the middle of the afternoon, Noah had three full buckets, and I'd reeled in an old shoe. It lay in the hot sun and smelled worse than everyone else's buckets lining the dock. I followed George's instructions and began to gut my catch, untying the laces and pulling out the insole. Fish eyeballs whizzed past my head, and something squishy thunked on my shirt.

At the opposite end of the pier, Noah pulled a fish from his bucket and pressed his knife against the tailfin, but the fish flopped, and Noah jumped and dropped his knife. The fish plunked back into the lake with a small splash, and Noah glanced around to see if anyone had noticed. I looked down, pretending to be fascinated by a bloated insole. Noah picked up the knife again and pulled a new fish from the bucket. He scrunched his face, raised the blade, and tried to hatchet the fish without looking, but he missed, and his knife jammed in the dock, and the fish flopped back into the water. Noah pulled the knife from the dock, tossed it by his bucket, and walked up to George. George nodded and pointed to the woods, and Noah walked toward a clump of trees. Noah had a badge for everything, and he couldn't gut a fish? He disappeared into the woods. I counted to ten and then walked over pools of ick to his end of the dock. No one paid attention as I reached into his bucket.

I worked fast. I sliced and filleted and arranged the fish in clumps because Noah wasn't neat, and rows would have looked suspicious. I washed the fish guts off the knife like George told us and then returned to my old shoe. I dunked my hands in the lake, and the silver scales floated off my hands like smelly, iridescent sequins. Before that day I'd never seen a fish that wasn't battered, stick shaped, and pulled from a box, but I knew a lot about knives because I spent my summers interning with the pencil factory's master sharpener, a former sushi chef who came to Ohio to escape the Yakuza. By the end of my training with Master Yamato, I could split my split ends into eighths. I pulled the insole from my shoe—sorry, Master Yamato—and did a crummy job slicing the bloated foam into one chunk, even though I could have filleted three or four paper-thin insoles.

Noah came back from the woods and looked at the clumps of cut fish and yelled, *George?* George misunderstood Noah's question to be a statement of completion and ordered the entire troop over to Noah's section of the dock. George marveled at Noah's work. He grabbed a fillet and held it out for us. *Now, boys, that's how you fillet a fish.* George glanced at the shoe I was holding and patted me on the head. *Keep trying, Frankie.* Noah searched his friend's faces and looked at their mangled catches. When he looked at me, I pointed at my bloated insole and shrugged my shoulders. I hoped he believed my blushing cheeks were just sunburned.

Mom picked me up at the end of the day, and as we drove away from the lake, she said three things: *Why do you smell like an old shoe? None of those boys could cut butter with a hot knife. Your prowess deserves to be recognized.* I looked out the car window and smiled, but I never said a word. I think the fact that I could fillet a fish and keep a secret made Noah think I was okay, so he started talking to me, and because he talked to me, the other boys stopped farting on my head, and that was all the recognition I wanted.

A few weeks ago, before I became a human pincushion, my troop started working on the subterfuge badge. Our guest speaker was a Vietnam vet who taught us tap code. Tap code is like Morse code, but you don't need a machine, you just tap on any hard surface. Prisoners of war in a place called the Hanoi Hilton used it. I thought Hiltons were fancy, but I guess that one was gross, no pool or TV but a lot of torture. The prisoners were in solitary confinement, and they wanted a way to talk to each other. It must be lonely to know that someone is on the other side of a wall, but they can't hear you. After we learned the basics, we divided into pairs. One person was the tapper and the other was the interpreter. We sat on opposite sides of the wheeled chalkboard, and George passed out words for us to practice. Noah was the tapper and I was the interpreter.

C-k-i-e? Do you mean cookie? I asked.

Noah tapped, Y-A-S.

I tapped, Y-O-U S-P-E-L-L-E-D I-T W-R-O-N-G.

It felt like a game, but the vet said we should take it seriously. He said it might save our lives. We spent the rest of the meeting practicing S-E-N-D H-E-L-P and T-O-R-T-U-R-E.

Sand hair turtle?

Torte? Like the dessert?

Do I like desert?

I stuck my head under the chalkboard's ledge. *Are you asking me if I like to eat hot sand?*

How could someone so cute be such a crappy speller? Before the meeting ended, Noah went off the word list and tapped Y-U

P-R-A-T-T-Y. When I decoded what he meant, I blushed and didn't bother correcting his misspelling.

Would Noah think I'm P-R-A-T-T-Y right now? Doubt it. I haven't seen myself because I can't shower until someone comes this afternoon to remove the tube that's stuck up my jellybox, and I think it's a widely accepted fact that it's hard to feel P-R-A-T-T-Y if you're peeing in a bag.

Mom walks in and sits on the edge of my bed. She's wearing a clean shirt, so today must not be yesterday, but maybe it's already tomorrow? When I wake up, I can't figure out if it's late-night dark or early-morning dark. The only way I figure it out is by looking at what's on TV, but someone keeps turning it off because no one hears me when I ask them to leave it on.

"How do you feel?" she asks.

I raise six fingers.

Mom forces a smile. "You're a lousy liar."

I pull one finger down. As a bag-peeing virgin with a gaping neck wound, I'm firmly a one, but Mom's strained smile tells me she could use a show of reassurance, so five it is.

"That's more like it!" she says.

She arranges my pillows and pats my head. I feel all five fingers plus her flat palm. Why can I feel her entire hand? Her eyes widen as I bring my hands to my head. Half of my head feels like its curly, broom-straw mess, but the other half feels like leg stubble, patchy and short-sharp. Mom pulls away my hands and wraps both of hers around mine. Oh no. This can't be good.

"The doctors were worried about infection. I'm so sorry. They wouldn't let me be in the operating room, and when I saw you in the ICU, they'd already cut some of your hair."

I grab my notebook. *SOME OF MY HAIR?*

Mom nods and reaches for a tissue. I run my hand across my head, then write, *Mirror?*

"Are you sure?"

I nod.

Mom pulls a compact from her purse, and my fingers shake as I lift the round lid. Cocksuckermotherfuckerdouchebag. I'm half Yule Brynner, half Phyllis Diller. Mom reaches for the box of tissues. My bald side is so white, a plain bagel with a schmear. I snap the compact shut and return it to Mom and write, *What happened to your hands?*

"The accident." She pauses. "Don't you want to talk about your hair?"

I shake my head. The difference between tragedy and triage is information, and Mom can't give me what I need. She doesn't paint her nails or wear makeup. The only reason she has a compact in her purse is because she got tired of other people being embarrassed when she had food in her teeth. The morning of the rally, I asked if she was going to wear lipstick since she was going to be on TV, but she shook her head and pointed to her face. "Nope. This is what a real woman looks like, and women need to see someone real. Everyone is too used to those fake women on *Woeful Valley*."

Woeful Valley is my favorite soap opera and Mom's idea of everything that's wrong with womanhood. When she found out that I wasn't at Quiz Bowl practice and was instead watching *Woeful Valley* at my friend's house, she didn't ground me; she sent my friend's mom a copy of *The Second Sex* and left a copy of *Our Bodies, Our Selves* on my bed with a hand mirror and a note:

1. Find your clitoris because a man never will.

2. Have bigger dreams than a life of lingerie and high-heeled marabou slippers.

I'll have to solve this hairtastrophe on my own. Mom doesn't look like she can handle one more worry anyway. I tilt the notebook toward her, *At least you have your hair.*

She takes the notebook, and as she writes, her shoulders shake, and her nose drips on the paper. I can't watch, so I stare at the ceiling. I've become an expert in counting the holes in the ceiling tiles.

#4. Pro: Improving math skills even in the hospital.

Mom blows her nose and rests the pad in my lap: *At least I have you.*

I lean my head on her shoulder and close my eyes.

"I'll buy you a hat," she offers.

Paper bag? I reply.

More tears.

You're a sap.

She kisses a bald spot. Her tears roll down the back of my neck. "I don't know what I did to deserve you."

We stay like that, hair to no hair, until Mom stops crying, and I can hear the beep-beep-beep machine again. I write and then nudge her. *Does Noah know?*

"Sweetie, the whole town knows. Oh, I forgot. Noah dropped something off while you were in intensive care."

She walks to the windowsill as I scrawl, *Has he seen me like this???* I bang my hand against the swing-out tray. Mom pulls a large brown envelope from her overnight bag and tucks it under her arm.

A doctor leans in the doorway. "Mrs. Rosenblum, can I speak with you?"

I write, *Ms.!* and turn the paper toward him, but he leaves the room. Mom takes the envelope with her. I slump on the pillow and try to move the clown balloon with my mind, and when that fails, I restart counting the ceiling-tile holes.

Before we learned about tap code, the troop learned about radar. Radar transmits waves that bounce off an object and then return as an echo. The echo describes the object's location, shape, and size, so if you learn to read the echo, you can figure out what the object is. It's like shaking Hanukkah gifts and trying to figure out if it's a box of socks or a book. My troop didn't have any real radar equipment, so George made us count off *one, two, one, two*, and we piled in the van and went to a cave on the edge of town. All the ones got bells, and the twos had to find the number ones based on their bell echoes. We weren't allowed to talk or use our headlamps, so everyone kept bumping into each other. When Noah bumped into me, I cupped my hands around my bell to muffle it, and I stood still, breathing in his deep-end-of-the-swimming-pool-and-campfire smell. If he found me, the game would be over, and I wanted him to stay where he was, pressed against me in the dark.

You cold? he whispered.

How did he know it was me? I had goose bumps but not because I was cold.

Yeah, I answered.

He wrapped his hand around mine and put the bell on the floor of the cave and then pulled off his sweatshirt. He reached for my elbows and raised my arms, slipped his sweatshirt over my head, the rustle of fleece fuzz and hair, and then he leaned in and brushed his lips against mine. I wrapped my arms around his neck, and he pulled me close, and as I pressed my mouth against his, I felt his chest beat against mine—an echo serenade. It wasn't how the manual described it, but that's how I understood radar. He never asked for his sweatshirt back. That's how I knew he liked me.

Mom comes in from the hall, and she's crying. Rosenblum women are not graceful criers. We wail and puff and splotch. We don't have glamorous, single teardrops like the women on *Woeful Valley*. Mom drops the envelope from Noah on the chair. It's out of my reach, but I try to grab it anyway.

I tap, H-E-Y.

Mom forces a smile. "Why do you keep tapping your fingers?"

She looks at my fingers and worry spreads across her already anxious face. She keeps smiling, but her lip quivers. She reaches for the plastic pitcher on the nightstand and pours a cup of water. She tilts the cup and swallows. My mouth waters. I'm not ready for liquids yet; they just squirt out of my neck hole. Mom peers over the cup's lip. "Sorry." She throws the cup in the trash and apologizes for never buying me dolls, for not bringing home a puppy when I asked for one, instead suggesting I become a veterinarian, and for buying cupcakes instead of making them like the other school moms. She apologizes for sending her secretary, Ron, to my school functions because she was too busy running a factory. She apologizes for making me intern with the head sharpener instead of sending me to summer camp. And when she finishes apologizing for all the things she didn't do, she wipes her nose on her bandages and apologizes for all the things she did do.

She apologizes for making me ride in the pencil van while she delivered pencils all night. She's sorry for embarrassing me when I got my first period. To celebrate we went out to dinner, and when the waiter asked if we really needed an extra-large pizza for just the two of us, Mom grabbed his arm and shouted loud enough for the entire restaurant to hear, *Yes! She's a woman now!* Mom blows her nose and keeps going. "I probably overreacted about Forest Nymphs. Maybe I shouldn't have pushed you to join Patriot Adventurers. I shouldn't have written the governor. If you wanted to sell cookies and wear a sash, that should have been fine with me. And, maybe I should have given you a girl's name. It's just . . . I thought . . . with a boy's name, you'd be spared the telescoping options of being a woman. I wanted you to have freedom, to mess up, to reinvent yourself, the kind of freedom that only men get."

I wrap my arms around her, and when she stops sobbing, I kiss her cheek, and do the only thing I can: raise both of my thumbs. Mom smiles, then walks to the bathroom. I tap on the swing-out tray, and she turns around. I point to the TV.

"You want it on?"

I nod my head.

Mom thinks that turning the faucet on full blast covers the sound of her crying. She closes the bathroom door, and the tap squeaks, and water gushes. The television screen warms up, changing from black to green and then color. A woman wearing a white shirt tucked into white pants runs through a field of daisies. The male voice-over says, "No leaks! Finally, you'll feel secure."

Mom remembers the envelope from Noah as she leaves for dinner. She puts it on the swing-out tray and kisses one of my bald patches. Once she's out the door, I count her footsteps. She stops at the nurses' station, then waits in front of the elevator, and as soon as the elevator dings, I grab the envelope. *Frankie Rosenblum, Room 421.* I love seeing how other people write my name. It makes me imagine myself differently. I trace my finger over Noah's *F* and *k*, and the hair on my arms stands up. I'm in the cave, wearing his sweatshirt, my lips pressed against his. I slide my finger under the tape and open the envelope and pull out a Bee Gees T-shirt and a piece of notebook paper folded in half.

> *Dear Frankie,*
> *I never said thank you for the fish thing. So, I'm saying it now.*
>> *Hurry up and get out of the hospital.*
>> *I miss your face,*
>> *Noah*

It's the T-shirt he was wearing under his Adventurer's uniform the day I filleted his fish. My IV tube tangles, but I manage to pull the shirt over my head. The Bee Gees are Noah's favorite band, and my least favorite band, but I fall asleep with Noah's shirt against my skin. Tonight, I love the Bee Gees.

RUTH

I haven't been to my storage space since my accident happened, but as I bend and try to raise the heavy door, my ulna remembers the night I'd like to forget. After Max died, this space was my refuge. Its brutal exterior and lack of windows offered structural reliability, a pause in the middle of a pell-mell spree. I kept the room sparsely furnished, just one table and a small sofa, because the walls were what gave me comfort. Picture by picture, I pierced thousands of images, overlapping other people's lives and other people's happiness.

Grief is a trickster. I expected sadness; I didn't expect transmutation, I didn't expect to look in a mirror and not recognize my own face, I didn't expect to look at a red recliner and wail.

In those first months after he died, I slept underneath a schizophrenic duvet of pinstripe suits and plaid golf pants. I thought grief would be leaden, but the slightest thing blew me off course. All I wanted was to feel anchored, something I never desired until my life was halved. One suit couldn't replicate his weight, so I emptied his closet and scooped the undershirts and sweaters from his drawers, even his winter coat, and if I stayed very still, it wasn't like a body, but it was enough weight that I could close my eyes and almost sleep. When friends came over and asked about the pile, I said I was cleaning out his closet, and they believed me at first, but weeks became months, and my lies were as pilly as Max's sweaters. One sweater was too loose, but five sweaters felt plausible, a hug.

Sam suggested, *Someone else could use those clothes. Wouldn't that make you feel good?* I only gave in because I had to replace the air conditioner. I burned out the motor from wearing multiple sweaters and sleeping underneath three-piece suits all summer. I folded the pants that used to hold his legs and the suits still broad from his shoulders, and with one short phone call, they were taken away, and he was dead, again. This is widowhood, not one death, a thousand: When the dry cleaner called and wondered why Max hadn't picked up his shirts; when I finally threw away his toothbrush, razor, and the last crossword puzzle we worked together; when he kept getting mail. The first time I went to the doctor and had to choose: married, divorced, widowed. When solicitors called and asked, *Is Mr. Stanhope at home?* I used to take messages because I liked to pretend he was on a long trip, but now I've learned to say, *Mr. Stanhope is dead,* because it gets me off the phone quicker.

The night of my accident, I slipped on Max's blue shirt, poured one finger of Scotch, looked at his monogrammed cuffs, and said, *Miss you.* Scotch, the bottled murmurations of starlings, the courage of liquid starts, because beginnings are easier than middles; beginnings are definite and recognizable, sharp and bordered like a photograph's edge. But, middles are underdeveloped, time spent waiting to wipe clean and restart. The Scotch was telling me to wipe the walls clean and start over, unpin all the layers of images, and reclaim all the claimed time. So, I did. The walls were arranged by color, a flat photographic rainbow. I drained my glass and dragged the ladder to the red section. Stop signs, heart-shaped boxes of chocolate, a scraped and bleeding knee.

Oxblood, that's what the woman at the furniture store called it, but Max and I just said red, the color of his favorite recliner that sat in the corner of our den. The recliner was sized for one, but that never stopped us. I'd crawl into the recliner while Max was reading, and as we tipped backward, Max would kiss me and laugh. *To the floor?* We'd sex our way down, and it became a joke. When he left for business trips, I'd hold his suitcase hostage and ask, *Love me?*

To the floor, he'd say.

In the first month after he died, the recliner was reliable, the musk of his wool sweaters and warm shoulders, until the one night the chair smelled like me, my hair, my clothes. I flattened my face against the headrest and pressed my nose into the arms, I pushed into the tufted leather buttons, the brass tacks, but, nothing. I lifted the seat cushion, hoping for crumbs because he used to smear graham crackers with butter and snack in the chair on Sunday afternoons, but all I found were five pennies, a flattened tissue, and something that might have been a crumb. I held it on my tongue until it dissolved and slid down my throat, and then I ran to the bathroom and threw up. I tried, but no matter how many encyclopedias and bags of mulch I piled on top of myself, the chair refused to tip. I couldn't get anywhere near the floor.

In those months, late at night when a car drove past the house, and the headlights traced an arc on the bedroom ceiling, my pulse would race. *He's home.* I'd rush out of bed, but on my way to the front door, I'd pass the recliner, and as soon as I saw it, I remembered. There were days I'd walk by the recliner and remember dumb fights, like when I stomped off with the map, and we didn't speak the entire car ride home, or times I groused about Max not rinsing his shaving stubble out of the bathroom sink. But mostly I wondered where he was, and I wondered if I'd ever feel whole again. Grief isn't ballsy like cancer, there's no baldness, no cut-off breast. I looked normal at work, but in private I was talking to a bar of soap, the one he used the morning he died. It still had divots from his fingernails, as if he had grabbed it as it slipped from the dish. On bad days, I'd stand in the dry shower and rub the soap down my neck, across my nipples, and between my legs, and I didn't dare turn on the water until I'd resealed the soap in a glass jar.

I don't remember the last words I said to him. Were they loving? Cranky? Rushed? Was I my good self on his last day or just my quotidian self? I assumed there would be more words, and more time; time to fight, time to fuck, time to waste, time to go to brunch because this is how everyone lives until someone dies and you're forced into the interregnum between naive assumption and shitass truth. The day he died, I didn't die, but life as I knew it did. An inverse birthday and there are no candles for that, and there are no presents; it's not life, it's the part of the space flight that ends with an ocean plunge and the capsule bobbing in the sea. I'm back on earth, but all I see is unrelenting flatness and salt-soaked water.

It's also true that I lied. Any time I was at the storage space, I said I was at work because who would understand my attempts to gather enough stolen time to bring back my dead husband? On the one-year anniversary of his death, I poured lighter fluid on the grill and burned all the sympathy cards. Sympathy was useless, sympathy didn't help. The neighbors peered over the fence and asked what I was grilling, and I said, *Steak*. I put a classified ad in the paper and sold the recliner for ten bucks.

When I finished unpinning the red images, I pulled down the orange ones—the three-hundred-pound pumpkin from the state fair, kids with candy corn fangs shoved on their teeth, joke ransom letters made from circus peanuts. More Scotch and on to yellow: sunflowers, mistaken photographs of the sun, dangling bananas from unzipped pants. Green was the largest section: pine boughs, Easter grass, edged lawns. When I reached indigo, I was woozy, and I should have stopped, but I didn't. I unpinned lilac bushes and a close-up of someone wearing sparkly eyeshadow.

I refilled my glass one more time, and then I saw it. A photograph of Max in the very shirt I was wearing. I looked at my arm; I looked at the wall. Have you been here all along? I rushed up the rungs. I stepped on the part of the ladder that read, *Do not step*. The snapshot was hard to reach. It was almost on the ceiling. I stood on my tiptoes but couldn't reach. I braced my hand against the opposite wall and scooted the ladder by rocking my pelvis until the ladder pitched forward, and I grabbed the photograph. I've got you. The ladder jerked. Max's shirt cuff snagged on a staple. I flinched and tugged. A loud rip and cold ground. My mouth oozed something metallic. When I came to, the room was carnival ceilings and Tilt-A-Whirl floors. I raised my arm to stop the spinning, and pain slammed through my shoulder and shot down my arm. A knob of pale bone stuck out of Max's blue sleeve. I squinted at the wall clock, two a.m. Only one person would answer at this hour, but the pay phone was out in the parking lot. Earlier in the night I'd raised the storage door to get some fresh air, but the door was at breeze height, not exit height.

I don't remember how I opened the door, but I do remember that the phone booth, jaundiced under the parking lot's lights, felt as distant as wherever Max was. I leaned against the booth until the door accordioned, and the overhead light flickered on. The phone rang and rang, and I closed my eyes. The line picked up, and the operator said, "Collect call. Will you accept the charges?"

Sam mumbled yes, and the operator clicked and left the line.

"I think I broke my arm."

"Be there in twenty."

I stayed in the booth until I heard car wheels on gravel and saw the swoop of headlights as Sam turned into the parking lot.

He pulled as close to the phone booth as he could, and he put his arms around my waist, and helped me into the truck. "Purse inside?"

I nodded and leaned against the headrest and closed my eyes. He returned with my purse, and we drove toward the hospital. At the first red light, he pulled a handkerchief from the glove box.

"I thought I saw Max," I said.

"With that amount of Scotch, you shoulda seen Jesus."

The admitting clerk was on the phone, and her back was to the counter. Sam hit the bell. "Can you help us? She's in pain."

The clerk looked over the top of her glasses. "Aren't we all."

"I think I broke my arm."

She peered over the counter. "Looks like it."

She slid a clipboard of forms and a pencil across the counter. Sam wheeled me to the waiting room and filled out the forms, searching through my purse for the insurance card. At the bottom of the sheet was a line drawing of a body for notating the locations and severity of pain on a scale of 1 to 10. Sam looked at me. "Ten?"

I nodded. The nurse called my name, and Sam rolled me across the waiting room. She held up her clipboard, blocking Sam from going any farther. "Patients and family only."

I could hear the grin in Sam's voice when he said, "I go where Mother goes." He's used to charming his way into situations where he shouldn't be; it's one reason he's such a good photographer. The nurse eyed our different skin tones, mine dark and his pale. She put her hands on her hips, but Sam wheeled me around her and said, "Adoption. It's impolite to stare." He stayed with me through the X-ray and the tetanus shot. When the doctor walked in holding my X-ray, Sam kissed my forehead. "I'll be in the waiting room, Mom."

The pain meds had kicked in and I tried to smile, but all I could do was drool. The doctor pulled the curtain around me, and I closed my eyes, lulled by the sounds of professional purpose, metal drawers opening and closing, stools wheeling across the floor, and people saying medical terms I didn't understand. A nurse touched my shoulder. "That's good, Mrs. Stanhope, try to relax. Think of someplace nice."

Someplace nice. Our den. A lazy, sunny Sunday. Max and I are stretched out at opposite ends of the big red couch, our legs entwined as we read the newspaper. It doesn't take much, it barely takes anything. He turns a page, shifts his weight, or clears his throat the way he does when he's reading something complex, and I can't help myself. I drop my section on the rug and crawl over his legs and straddle him. He keeps reading because that's part of the game. I unbutton most, but not all, of my shirt because that's part of the game too. There's no point if it's too easy. He looks at me and holds his hands against my shirt until he finds the two small circles holding the shirt together, and then he leans forward and unbuttons them. I wrap one hand around the back of his neck and press the other against the cap of his shoulder, a push-pull. He traces the arc of my hipbones. He pulls the shirt down my arms but not all the way off. Newspaper rustles. My shoulder presses against the table; cold air hits my stomach. Max, why are your hands so cold? My eyes are heavy, but I see a glint of metal, something sharp. I try to grab his wrist, but my limbs are sloppy. I can't keep them upright. He chuckles. "We've got a live one here." The nurse holds my arms against the table. "I'm sorry, Mrs. Stanhope, we have to cut off your shirt."

I say, "No," but my voice doesn't make a sound. Cold metal scissors across my navel, the snip and rip of cotton sleeves and monogrammed cuffs, the ping as ten buttons land in a small dish.

ESTHER

Plungers are girthier than pencils. The corners of my mouth are raw from being so accommodating. My teeth are antsy, and my gums are plotting. Last night when I flossed, I'm pretty sure my molar moved.

I ring my lips with Vaseline, pour a drink, and balance the plunger's red cap on my knees to make the gnawing easier. I drink and gnaw through the *Late Movie*, and by the middle of the *Late Late Movie*, I neither notice nor care about the oily sheen and waxy flavor of my rum and Tab. When the TV station ends its broadcast day, and the bald eagle soars in front of the waving flag, I put my hand over my heart and stand for the national anthem. The plunger drops from my lap and rolls under the coffee table, and I fall backward onto the couch.

I wake up with my hair mashed to my cheek and my heart racing. I dreamed I had marshmallows for teeth. Fat, useless sugar tubes. My teeth couldn't crunch or bite or MouthFeel test anything. I reach for the glass, but the smell of rum makes my eyes water. I push it across the table and stare at the ceiling. I count backward and take long breaths. Calm mind, calm mouth. Ten, inhale, nine, exhale . . .

It's hard to control a mouth with a mind of its own. I never know what's happening inside my skinless bones.

Seven, exhale, six, inhale. I rub my eyes and lap my tongue around my mouth for reassurance, molar peaks and calcium stalactites, but

I keep imagining things that seem solid but aren't: sugar cubes, ice-covered lakes that yawn and swallow snow-suited toddlers.

Bad thoughts, bad bites, Esther.

What's strong? Steel? Tin? Why don't I know anything about metal? I should know more about metal. I will use my free time to learn about metals. The dentist suggested something called visualization. He told me to imagine myself walking through a forest. *Forests are relaxing*, he said.

Okay, here I go. Just me and acres of trees waiting to be cut and shaped into pencils, and since biting pencils is my favorite thing, this will be good. I mean I'm so good at biting pencils I get paid to do it. Oh, wait. I'm not getting paid. No bite, no buy, and it's bye-bye, car; bye-bye, apartment; and I'm gonna live on the street, and no one wears white pants when they live on the street, period or no period. Wait, I can live in the forest. No, grass stains. I wipe my eyes and stare at the ceiling. Start again. Five, exhale. Four, inhale. Three, exhale. This isn't working. I need to be something else, somewhere else. What's not a pencil? An eraser. Perfect. I'll clear my mind by clearing the forest. Two, inhale. One, exhale. I'm a big pink eraser. I prop myself against a trunk and rub its woody base until it disappears. I stroke up to the leafy canopy, but I can't concentrate. I keep falling off the trunk, and it's just wrong to erase wood right now. Try again, Esther. I put myself back in the forest and lean against a tree, but the giant eraser turns on me and starts erasing my feet.

I sit up and open my eyes. The light outside has changed from late-night secret to early-morning shame. What else do I like to do? I like swimming. What about the ocean? I turn over and move my arms off the side of the couch, like it's a giant surfboard. The breeze feels nice against my face; I smell salt as I paddle into the surf. Everything is good, I can do this. And then I see it, a shark fin. That's it! I can be a shark, the eraser of the ocean, all fierce gums and picket-fence teeth. If I'm a shark, I can bite anything, tin cans and speedboats and between-meal snacks of shins and surfboards. Screw the forest; I'm a shark.

Wait, if shark teeth are so strong, why do so many people wear them around their neck? If they were that strong, they wouldn't fall out, right? I swim down the hall and pull the *S* encyclopedia off the shelf.

> *Unlike human teeth, shark teeth are not very strong and tend to fall out easily. This is not problematic for sharks, because they constantly produce new teeth to replace the ones they lose.*

Falling out teeth, that's bad, but many teeth and replaceable teeth, that's good? I flop back on the couch in a dead-man's float. There's no point in anything. I might as well do chores.

I turn on the light and fold laundry and button clean shirts on to hangers. My closet is small, too small for a shark and too small for a forest, although the wooden hangers smell good. They smell like everything is in its place, like teeth that don't fall out and trees that sway but don't break. I slide to the floor and brace my feet against the wall and look at the undersides of hangers. It's easy to confuse biting and chewing because for most people one leads to the other. Chewing and swallowing are fine ways to stay alive, but the magic is in the bite, not the chew. A bite is pure, nothing but teeth-to-surface contact. Chewing messes everything up, textures change, surfaces break down, and everything devolves to mush.

I turn off the closet light, and after every wooden hanger is darkened by spit and pocked with bite marks, I curl on the floor and fall asleep, my mouth full of wool fuzz and cedar nubs.

RUTH

Frankie is out of intensive care, but the town remains in shock. The sudden closing of the pencil factory has left too many people with nothing to do and no place to go. The citizens of Lead don't leisure well; without the structure of daily work, they flail and ruin like a dropped roll of film. For the first week, bars increased their sales, but that was short lived because most of the town is descended from farmers, folks who tilled the earth and aligned their habits to the cadence of the sun. They're not the kind to day drink.

Customers wander into my shop, telling me they've flipped their mattresses and cleaned out their garages, but now what? Now that they have the time to do all the things they thought they'd do if they only had the time, they realize they don't care about those things. I suggest "Vacations? Trips to parents or in-laws?" But they shake their heads. Enjoying unexpected free time is boastful; it tempts fate, and worse than that, it means they aren't suffering enough about the accident. "How about planting a garden or enrolling in a photography class? Here's a coupon." They shuffle out of the store, heads down, without buying film.

Women who previously left the house fully coiffed are wearing shirts crusted in baby spit-up and pants flocked with dog hair. Being in public with rollers in your hair is no longer a cause for embarrassment. Out-of-work husbands could ease their wives' burdens by participating in the drudgery of wiping bottoms and decrusting jam sandwiches, but that's not what is happening. With their husbands underfoot, women have lost their sole proprietorship, the domestic front. After cold shoulders and additional ticks in the tally of wifely resentment, the women retreat to the supermarket and form cereal-aisle sanctuaries, where they whisper confessions and seek absolution from cardboard toucans. In garages and basements, projects are started in earnest but abandoned for lack of deadlines. The TV station modified programming to show movies about surmounting overwhelming odds and achieving impossible goals, and that worked for a while, but then people felt guilty about wasting so much time watching television. They have two legs and two arms, shouldn't they be doing something? The factory employs more men than women, but out-of-work women aren't faring much better than their male counterparts. Women with children are happy to spend more time with their kids, until all that time spent together makes them remember how much they enjoyed working. Single women experiment with things they thought housewives did, making aspic and handwashing hand washables, until they realized aspic is joyless gelatin, and they weren't missing a damn thing by eating cold cereal for dinner.

I find Juliet's spare key underneath the ceramic toad on the front porch. Juliet and I aren't particularly close, but not particularly close doesn't mean squat right now, and besides, I owe her. It's thanks to Juliet that *I'm alive*. I've known her since before Frankie was born and before her husband left, which means I've known her long enough to know she'll say she doesn't need help because that's what women like us say. That's what I said after Max died, and that's what I said as Juliet drove me home after the manager of the grocery store called the police because I was spitting on all the lettuce.

Juliet's foyer is strewn with weeks of bills and cards that sailed through the mail slot and scattered because no one is here to pick them up. Grocery store flyers and newspapers go in the trash, and the rest I sort in descending urgency. The couch in the den is the kind that's seen a lot of naps, and the glass ashtray on the coffee table is clearly not decorative. Beside the ashtray is a half-empty can of Tab, a pack of cigarettes, and two encyclopedias with index cards marking pages. Houses should look like this, peppered with the mess of a full life. The older I get the less I care about tidying anything. Life is short; go swimming.

I've never been in Juliet's kitchen, but the gestures of domesticity are predictable, and I find her rubber gloves under the sink. I scrape a bowl of moldy oatmeal into the garbage disposal, drain the percolator, dump the ashtray, put the box of Crunch Berries cereal into the cabinet, and load the dishwasher. It clanks while I cull rotten food from the fridge and drag the trash to the curb. I scrub and wipe until the sink is clean and the faucets are shiny, something I never do at home because spot-free faucets are a tremendous waste of time, but most people like such nonsense, and in times like this, nonsense can be the one thing that gets you through.

At Max's funeral Juliet told me that no one rends their clothes anymore. Instead mourners pin a remnant of politely ripped black cloth to their funeral suit. That was the stupidest thing I'd ever heard. Mourning can't be distilled. After the service and after shiva, when I was alone with a refrigerator full of casseroles I wouldn't eat, I ripped my nightgown and didn't leave our bed. I didn't want visitors, but they came anyway. Sam picked up my newspapers and put out fresh water for the cat. It was high summer, and neighbors left garden tomatoes and paper sacks of runner beans with handwritten notes, *Already strung!* When they returned the following week to find tomato sludge and fruit fly colonies helicoptering over the beans, they'd clean up the mess and leave zucchini instead. Blackberries, eggplant, cucumbers, it didn't matter. The chirpy vitality of summer was anathema. I ate saltines; I wished I were dead.

Under the sink in Juliet's bathroom, I find a can of scouring powder and another pair of rubber gloves. When Frankie comes home, everyone will bring casseroles and pies, but no one will scrub the toilet or clean the tub because cleaning toilets isn't boastful like piecrust rosettes, but when life's cruelty kicks you in the teeth, it's best to not see black mold growing in your grout. I shake green powder in the tub, bend over, and scrub.

When Juliet found me in the produce aisle, I was wearing my ripped nightgown and Max's college sweatshirt, the one I slept in when he was out of town. Juliet later told me I was also wearing Max's wool cap. I don't remember that, but I do remember being cold even though it was July. By the time Juliet arrived, several customers had already reported me to the store manager, and when he asked me to stop, I looked at him and said, *You stop*. I stood, hands on my hips, long strings of spit rappelling from my lips and landing on the pale, secretive heads of iceberg lettuce. I'd moved to the oblong rows of romaine when Juliet pried my hands from my hips and wrapped them around a shopping cart. She touched the middle of my back and whispered, *Push*. The cashier had a puzzled expression as she pointed at my empty cart, but Juliet handed her a twenty and said, *Mind your own business and throw away all the lettuce*.

Juliet drove to my house with the windows down and parked by the curb. She drew a hot bath and told me to get in. She left the bathroom door open, and I sat in hot water and stared at black mold growing in the grout of my pink tile. Out in the hall, I heard the swish of fabric being pulled off mirrors. Juliet returned with a plastic cup, rolled up her sleeves, and knelt on the bath mat. She poured shampoo and rubbed her fingertips through my filthy hair.

To the outside world, Max and I were fiercely independent people, but at night we curled around each other like a shoreline. He mapped me, claiming the junction of my jaw and neck, cresting my clavicle's ridge, his tongue salty from the sea of my upper thighs. Most nights I fell asleep as he raked his fingers along the contour where forehead becomes scalp. When Juliet lathered the same spot and it didn't feel the same, I heaved like a child. My own territories had seceded, and it's a terrible thing to be homesick and still at home. Juliet was steady and quiet, pressing a soft washcloth over my eyes and tipping my head into her hand while she rinsed my hair. She wrapped me in a towel and dried my skin, clipped my toenails, and lotioned my cracked heels. She wiped the steam from the mirror and combed the snarls from my hair, and then she put her hands on my bare shoulders and said, *Ruth, enough's enough. You're alive. That's all you've got, and it's got to be enough.*

I started with the mirror by the front door. In its small oval face I lied to myself: I'm alive. After I'd practiced enough to convince my lips and chin—all the tiny mirror would reflect—I moved on to bigger mirrors. On bad days I sat in front of the toaster and fought back: No, you're not. The last mirror, the wide one above our dresser, was the hardest because to see my reflection I had to look at our bed.

Businesses don't run themselves, so I returned to work. When anyone asked me how I was, which they asked incessantly because they didn't know what else to ask, I said, *I'm alive.* People assumed my response indicated gratitude, but that's not what I meant. It wasn't optimistic, it was an undeniable fact: I'm alive; he's not.

The tub shines and the grout's been scrubbed. I shake green powder into the toilet, scrub, and tap the toilet brush on the side of the bowl. The only thing left to clean is the mirror above the sink. I spray blue cleaner and wipe with a paper towel, and when there are no streaks, I point my rubber glove at the old woman in the mirror and say, "Still alive." I lock the front door and slip the key back under the ceramic toad and wonder what two words I can give Juliet.

I drive to the Vixen by the lake and sit in the camera obscura to think. The factory burning isn't our first hardship. We've seen twisters rip through trailer parks, and the soybean blight of 1962 sent farmers into church basements to accept food grown by amateurs.

Before the accident we rubbed our eyes, blew our noses, and baked casseroles for each other because we knew that misery is nothing if not generous, and maybe it's because we suffer winters under elephant skies, or maybe because Lead is rich with visitors who navigate with their wits and white canes, but we've always gotten on with life because there's no other option, and while everyone is permitted some intermittent pauses, all-out torpor is downright shameful. Individuals have rallied for individuals, and families have rallied for families, and churches will rally for congregations of different gods, but the entire town has never had to rally for itself. The factory affects all of us, all at once. It's too much to suffer and simultaneously comfort the suffering; that's like being in two places at once, and the only thing that can do that is light.

I can't rebuild the factory, but maybe I can change how we see. I spread a blanket on the floor and wait while my eyes adjust. The moon rises like milk, spilled on the lake. I look at the waves and count my breath in threes. An uncommon mantra, but it's mine: developer, stop, fix—the trinity of photographic chemicals that transform a negative into a positive. Developer is the summoner, chemically coaxing the memory of witnessed light—summer rays on surf and bare feet dangling over a dock, flashlights swung in tents, strands of colored lights tossed in pine trees softened by snow. Developer is the chemical everyone knows, but fixer is the most important because it makes film safe to be in daylight. On the ceiling the waves crest and the milk swells. My breathing is long and slow, and my lids are heavy.

I wake up, and the moon is gone. The lake is paused overhead, a still, dark slab. Don't be the lake, Ruthie.

And that's when I realize the answer has been there all along, just waiting for me to see it. Photographic fixer, the third chemical in the developing process. Fix stabilizes negatives and makes them safe to be seen in daylight. A negative that's fixed is productive; it can be printed and turned into a positive. Fix is what the town needs. Our present is lousy, our future is uncertain, but our past is still good. Maybe I can use the past to invigorate people about their future. All the present images are sad: the neon sign that can't write because the town is all wrong, but images of past joy might bolster future happiness.

I call Sam, and he offers to help in whatever way he can. I call suppliers and order specialized equipment and train my staff in photo-restoration techniques. Over the next weeks I consult experts in hand tinting and tintype restoration. I research the optimum way to pry apart photographs stored in plastic albums and ignored in hot attics. I pass the mirror by the front door and I forget to say I'm alive, because I don't have to convince myself. I imagine how happy people will be when they drop off damaged photographs and pick up restored versions of their past.

I rent billboards and record radio spots. I hire a director who makes a television commercial staring a former Miss Ohio and an actor in a full-body vixen suit. Furry paw in manicured hand, they smile for the camera and say, "Vixen fixes your past!"

ESTHER

Frankie is wearing headphones, and she's turned away from the door, a skinny lump underneath stiff hospital blankets. Bouquets of roses line the windowsill. I tiptoe to the bed, making my best goofball face. It takes two coughs and one ahem, but when she finally rolls over, she opens her arms in a big hug. It's hard to hold her without tangling in her tubes, but I do my best.

"Nice hair, Miss Cellaneous."

She gives me a thumbs-up and pats the side of the bed. I kick off my sandals and scoot next to her.

"Don't these people know your position on roses?"

Frankie shakes her head, opens a notebook, and puts it on my lap.

1. Soooooooooooooooooooooooo happy to see you!

2. This place sucks eggs.

3. I'm bored.

4. Are you OK?

I laugh at the second one and squeeze her hand. "How could you not be?" is my answer to number three, and when I read the fourth one I clench my jaw because I don't want to cry. I lean my head on hers. "I'm fine. How are you?" She raises her eyebrows, turns the page, and points to something she's already written.

Don't bullshit the bullshitter.

"Efficient," I say.

I reach for the notebook, but she pulls it back and flips a few pages. "What else you got in that magic book?" I ask.

She turns to another page. *For me to know and you to find out.*

As she writes, I laugh and lean against the pillow. The beeping machines, the IV bag dripping into her arm, all the roses. I slide off the bed and walk to the window. Down in the parking lot a young woman helps an elderly woman out of her wheelchair and into the passenger seat of a car. The bunch of roses nearest to me is pale pink. I pluck one petal and then another and then another. The young woman closes the passenger door and walks around the back of the car. She stops and leans against the trunk and looks up. I don't know if she can see me, but just in case she can, I wave. Her shoulders shake, and she puts her hands on her knees and leans over. Through the window I touch her small brown head. Stupid roses. I pluck and pull until one vase is nothing but stems. Twenty more vases. I turn toward Frankie. "Want to play a game?" She nods and keeps writing. The woman outside wipes her eyes, tucks her hair behind one ear, and opens the driver's-side door. I pull out my shirttail and pluck rose petals until my shirt pouch is full and fragrant. When the young woman pulls out of the parking lot, there's one bouquet left. "Ready?"

Frankie nods.

I jump on the bed and throw handfuls of petals into the air. They scatter across the stiff sheets stamped with the hospital logo. Frankie's eyes widen, and she claps and scissors her feet under the sheets so the petals hop and tumble to the floor. I scoop and arrange them on her partially bald head like a floppy crown. She raises her pencil in the air like a scepter, and I curtsey on the bed. "Is Your Majesty pleased?" She throws her arms out for a hug and pats the bed, so I squeeze in, and we flutter-kick rose petals. She hands me the notebook. *I know it's hard for you.*

"What do you mean?"

Frankie taps the pencil against my jaw. Bandages wrap around her neck, and the room smells like rubbing alcohol and sour flower water.

"No. It's been a good break. Really! I cleaned my refrigerator, and handwashed my hand washables. I made soup and even reordered my closet. I'm thinking about buying those fancy padded hangers."

She scribbles, *Liar*, then flips a few pages.

A List for Esther

1. Bobby pins

"The metal makes my filings zing," I say. Frankie scrunches her brows and points to the next item.

2. Phone book

"Made me look like I was applying black lipstick during a car crash." She crosses out the phone book.

3. Your brisket

"Seriously? It's that bad?"

She turns to her *Yes* page.

"Fine. I'll never have you over for brisket again." She points to the tube sticking in her neck and then uses the back of her hand to mop her brow in fake relief.

4. Celery

"Useless vegetable."

A pox on the vegetable kingdom, she writes.

"Indeed."

A nurse pops her head in the doorway. "I'm sorry, visiting hours are over."

Frankie loops her arm through mine. I turn to the nurse. "I'm sorry, looks like I have to stay."

The nurse shakes her head. I turn to Frankie and shake my head and point at the nurse. Frankie leans as far as her tubes will allow and nods yes, but the nurse says, "Sorry, Frankie, nice try."

I slide off the bed and buckle my sandals as slowly as I can. "You want anything, kiddo?"

Frankie points to the television. I turn it on, and while it warms up, I kick rose petals under the bed so Frankie won't get in trouble. A maxi pad commercial comes on, the one with the woman in white pants, running through a field of daisies. Frankie scribbles, and before she can tilt the notebook in my direction, I say, "Who the hell wears white pants on their period?"

She tilts the notebook in my direction. *Who the hell runs through fields of daisies?*

"You want some music? A book? More roses?"

She shakes her head and reaches for my arm and holds it tight. Her pencil scratches the paper. *I don't like feeling this way.*

"Are you in pain? I can get the nurse. Let me get the nurse."

Frankie writes, and I turn toward the door, but she yanks my sleeve. *Helpless.*

I lean over and wrap my arms around her. "I know. You're too good for this dump, Miss Cellaneous."

A nurse enters the room carrying a stainless steel tray with gauze and a large needle. I hug Frankie tighter and curl my toes in my sandals because I don't want to cry in front of her. I walk backward, waving with both arms, until the nurse points at her watch and closes the door.

I stand in the noisy hall and stare at Frankie's closed door. It takes me a few minutes before I'm composed enough to walk to the elevator. On the way, I pass the nurses' station. Over the intercom a code blue is called, and the nurses rush toward the other end of the hall. I look both ways, then reach over the counter and dump an entire container of tongue depressors into my purse. I push the elevator button again and again until the doors open, and then I stand in the corner, holding my bulging purse against my ribs so it won't pop open. The elevator doors take their time. I avoid my reflection in the chrome and watch the lighted numbers count down to "Lobby." I exit the hospital like my purse isn't full of contraband wood, and then I run through the parking lot, get in my car, slam the door, and shift into reverse. I catch my reflection in the rearview mirror. Tongue depressors on each side of my mouth, ramps going nowhere, fast. I will not buy more plungers. I will not listen to another lecture on my diet from the hardware store clerk. I will stay out of my closet. These are great. Everything is going to be fine.

By the time I get home, the tongue depressors' smooth exteriors have revealed their splintery, sham souls.

Two rum and Tabs later, the stereo is up to ten, and I'm exercising. I open dresser drawers, pull ceiling fan chains, turn doorknobs, and flip light switches—all with my teeth. I rearrange the stuff on my coffee table and organize my *People* magazines in alphabetical order according to the last name of the cover celebrity. When my drool starts to warp the glossy paper, I hold a paper towel between my front teeth and blot. I work up an appetite. My teeth pull a turkey potpie out of the freezer and set the oven to 425 degrees. I set the dinner table. Bread plate, dinner plate, soup bowl, spoon, fork, knife, water glass, wineglass, teacup and saucer, napkin folded and presented in a wooden napkin ring. The one place setting looks so good I decide to set the entire table. I have more plates than room for plates, so I go to the basement and get the table leaf and the two extra chairs. The table legs are delicious, but I've got a throbbing crick in my neck from bending at weird angles.

While the potpie cooks, I inventory my apartment's rigidity. I rummage through junk drawers hoping to find a pencil, but all I find are rubber bands (too thin), one old peppermint candy fused to its wrapper, one taper candle (waxy regret), coupons clipped but forgotten (too slick), and five matchbooks. Ice cubes are the desired hardness, but the cold makes my teeth zing; however, the ice tray is surprisingly satisfying. Under the kitchen sink, a cluster of dry sponges looks promising, but they taste like Comet. The iron skillet tastes like old bacon, which isn't entirely unpleasant, and the Sunday paper, while encouragingly thick, is fundamentally weak, yielding to the smallest bit of saliva, and lipsticking my mouth in green and red smears because ground chuck and broccoli are on sale at the Food Barn. The oven timer buzzes, and

I wrap a kitchen towel around my neck, put the potpie on the counter to cool, and begin to bob and weave like a boxer. I hold my boobs and jab at my opponent in the kitchen window. The potpie steam makes me look like I've worked up a sweat. Champ, you got this. You can last thirty days. People without legs run marathons. Mothers pull cars off their babies. I punch my reflection. Who runs marathons without legs? How do you even do that? I don't have a kid. And no job means no health insurance, and no insurance means no dentist, and no dentist means my teeth will fall out, and no teeth means no boyfriend, and no boyfriend means no baby, so it looks like I'll die alone, and no one will find me until cats eat my face. I throw the towel at the window. I don't have a cat.

It's time for *Woeful Valley*. I flop on the couch and eat potpie while the intro music plays. Sarah is out of her coma! She's awake and propped up in a hospital bed, wearing a delicate robe, her hair falling across the pillow in blonde waves. Sarah waking up from a five-year coma looks better than I ever have. My sweatpants have odd, oily stains on the thighs, and the waist elastic is so stretched I had to tie it in a large, lumpy knot, otherwise my pants fall down. Sarah has a plan. All the women on *Woeful Valley* have plans. I need a plan. The women of *Woeful Valley* have husbands and ex-husbands and bartender/pool boy/gardener lovers that they greet at the door, wearing high-heeled marabou slippers. Maybe I should get a boyfriend. Or some bedroom slippers. Sarah's husband strokes her hair and calls her darling. I stroke my own hair. It's awkward. He hides a bouquet of roses behind his back, and when he swoops them in front and gives them to her, she cries a single, perfect tear. I sob into my potpie and make new stains on my sweatpants.

The episode ends, and the theme music plays, and I want dessert. I walk to the bathroom, remove the toilet paper from the roll, and wedge the ceramic toilet paper holder in my mouth.

Back in the kitchen I start washing the dishes, but it takes me longer than usual because my palms are itchy and my tongue is numb and starting to swell. I hope I'm not allergic to faux-colonial dinette sets. My kitchen window overlooks the apartment parking lot and a scrubby field. Down in the field, the cute guy who drives the Monte Carlo is playing Frisbee with his dog. The dog leaps and catches the Frisbee in his big white teeth.

Cute dog and his cuter owner exchange the Frisbee a few more times until the dog catches the disc in midair and refuses to release it. Cute Guy walks to his dog and tugs on the disc, but the dog won't give it up. I rinse a plate and imagine that if Cute Guy and I ever met, we'd have so much to talk about. His dog's teeth won't release; my teeth won't release. Cute Guy drags the dog around by the Frisbee until the dog sits on his haunches and refuses to move. Cute Guy digs in his pocket, pulls out a treat; the dog's ears perk up and he drops the Frisbee. Cute Guy pats the dog's head, picks up the Frisbee, and sails it into the air, and the dog runs, tail wagging. A boyfriend. I stand on my tiptoes in imaginary high-heeled bedroom slippers. My jaw unclenches. The toilet paper holder falls into the sink and breaks.

FRANKIE

The phone rings, and I pick up the receiver.

"Hello?"

I press the phone closer. *Hello.*

"Hello? Hello?"

I thrust the phone at Mom. She holds the receiver and answers without thinking, because answering a phone is the dumbest thing in the world: all you have to do is open your mouth and sound falls out.

"Hello? Oh, hi. She's . . . well . . . it's day by day. No, not yet. Maybe in six months? Extensive rehabilitation, yes."

I hate it when she talks about me like I'm not here.

"You want what? Okay. Why?"

I grab the notebook and scribble, *I CAN HEAR YOU!*

Before the accident my handwriting was neat. Compact ascenders and generous descenders, but now I write in big blocks because otherwise no one listens. I tap on Mom's back: T-U-R-N A-R-O-U-N-D.

"No, I doubt I'll ever open it again. Hold on, let me check." She cradles the phone between her ear and shoulder. "It's George. Would you like the troop to visit?"

I nod my head and write *yes* and underline it until I run out of room on the page. If the troop visits, Noah visits. Mom arranges the details, then sits on the edge of the bed.

"George wants a pair of your shoes."

Shoes?

"I don't understand it either, but he wants me to drop them off tonight. Mind if I leave a bit early?"

I give her the thumbs-up.

A few nights ago I begged Mom to stop sleeping in the brown recliner. I know she wants to be near me, but it creeps me out to be watched while I sleep. I know she's worried, but she can't give me what I need: a good haircut and some space. Space to be sad or worried or angry or bored or all of those, all at once. Mom's too wigged-out because the entire town depends on her, and she thinks the accident is her fault, and no matter how many times I hold up the *This is not your fault!* page, she gets all bleary-eyed and clingy and wants to hold my hand and tell me everything is going to be okay, which we both know is total bullshit. My friends' moms taught their daughters to say *please* and *thank you*, but Mom didn't care about being polite; she taught me that *a woman must seize her own island*, but islands of laryngeal trauma and half-bald heads can't be seized, and besides I sunburn easily and get seasick. I just need time to get used to the fact that I can't talk yet.

Who knows why George wants a pair of my shoes, but I need Mom to go home, otherwise Nurse Paul won't hang out in my room. Most of the nurses seem scared of Mom or they feel bad for her, but either way they don't talk the same to me when she's around. Nurse Paul is the only one who lets me just feel. He doesn't try to solve anything. Sometimes at the end of his shift, he comes to check on me, and we listen to Iggy or Nico, and he doesn't think my love for punk means that I'm mad or sad, even though some nights I'm both, and some nights I'm neither. I just want to listen to music and not think about the fact that Noah will dump me and I'll have to go to prom alone with my IV pole, and even though prom is the dumbest, it's one thing to mock prom with your boyfriend, and it's another thing to not even be able to talk about how stupid it is.

Mom usually hangs around until I'm ready to fall asleep, and then she goes to the cafeteria, comes back with coffee, and stares out the window and picks chunks of Styrofoam off her cup. The coffee smell wakes me up, so I stare at Mom staring out the window, neither of us sleeping.

I fake yawn and flip to my *Tired!* page, then close my eyes while she gathers her purse. I count her steps to the hall, and when the elevator dings and the doors close, I fling off the covers and get out of bed in search of help. I can hide my hospital gown by pulling up my blankets, but unless I wear a bag on my head, I can't hide this fifth-floor hair— that's the floor where the loony patients are.

Most of the nurses watch *Woeful Valley*, and they'll update me on the latest episodes when Mom isn't around. I wheel my pole to the nurses' station, and the night nurse looks up from a pile of charts. "Hi, Frankie, how do you feel tonight?"

I hold up five fingers.

She smiles. "Not bad. Ready for your update?"

I nod.

"Two days ago Sarah came out of her coma only to discover she's not Sarah, she's Sarah's twin sister, Lucy, and the person she thought was Lucy was actually her husband dressed as a woman, and that's who hypnotized her into robbing the bank."

I tuck my notebook under my arm, throw both hands in the air and wiggle all my fingers.

"I know! Who would have guessed her sister was a he pretending to be a she just to rob a bank! Need anything else?" she asks.

I point to the list of doctors and nurses and tap on Paul's name.

"On break." And she points to the nurses' lounge at the end of hall.

I push my pole down the hall, open the lounge door, and snap my fingers to announce myself. Everyone puts their sandwiches in their laps and raises their hands, describing their day using the finger scale. Mostly sixes and sevens. They point to me. I put my notebook between my knees, gesture to my bandaged neck, and hold up six fingers, and then I point to my half-shaved head and hold up two balled fists, zero fingers. I raise my notebook in front of my face: *Noah. Tomorrow! Hair?*

Paul finishes chewing something that looks like baloney and cheese on white bread. "You need Sue." He points to a nurse who looks like Farrah Fawcett. I've seen her before; she's changed my IV bag in the middle of the night, and it's hard to forget her determined feathers. I look at my slippers and grip my IV pole. Farrah/Sue's blue eyeshadow and voluminous feathery fringe isn't getting anywhere near my head. What gesture means *No, no, thank you, hell no?* Before I figure that out, she's standing in front of me, surveying the mess on my head. She circles me once, twice, and on the third time presses her forehead into mine. I smell egg salad.

"Just because I look like Farrah Fawcett doesn't mean I think you should." She runs her fingers through what's left of my hair, steps back, and points at Paul. "This will take a while. Do my rounds?"

Paul looks at me and nods. "Anything for my favorite mute." He comes over and ruffles my hair. "Don't worry, you're in good hands."

I shrug my shoulders. If Paul trusts her, I trust . . . well, okay, I'm afraid of Farrah/Sue making my hair look like hers, but on the scale of things I fear, I'm more afraid of looking like something that an owl barfed, so I give two thumbs-up and she claps.

"Righteous!" She turns to Paul. "I need a dozen eggs, two metal bowls, a cold Tab, and a whisk."

"A whisk?" Paul asks.

"Darlene in the cafeteria. Stat!"

Farrah guides my IV pole into the bathroom and helps me sit on the edge of the tub. She kneels so we're at eye level. "You're going to love it." I don't know if that's a threat or a promise, but I sit tight until she returns with a big paint-splattered duffel bag that she tosses on the floor and unpacks. Shampoo, conditioner, a can of hair spray taller than my head, four combs, a pair of scissors, electric clippers, a rubber-banded wad of bobby pins, two packs of Fruit Stripe gum, a cigarette lighter, and a hair dryer. She arranges her tools on the counter like she's prepping for surgery, and when she sees my expression she laughs. "Hazard of the job. You should see my sock drawer." She pops three pieces of Fruit Stripe into her mouth, wraps a towel around my neck, and supports my head while she scrubs and lathers what's left of my hair. Her hands are soft, and the bathroom begins to smell like grape Fruit Stripe and apple shampoo. She hums and squirts conditioner, rubbing my hair from ends to roots.

She rinses and begins combing out my tangles. Paul stands at the bathroom door with a straw between his teeth, balancing a carton of eggs, two bowls, a whisk, and a can of Tab. He places the eggs on the toilet tank and the bowls on the seat, then opens the Tab, plops in the straw, and hands it to Farrah with a kiss. I smack my foot against the edge of the tub. She smiles. "Should we tell her we went to the MC5 concert together?" Paul grins while Farrah turbans a towel around my head and puts her hands on her hips. "You can't judge a girl by her hair. Not even hair as fine as this." She executes a perfect Farrah flip-smile combo. Paul laughs, and I bang my hands against the edge of the tub in glee. She opens the egg carton. "More." Paul raises his eyebrows, but Farrah raises hers higher, and Paul laughs and says, "Got it. More." He leaves the bathroom.

Farrah reaches into her bag and pulls out the electric clippers. My eyes widen. She puts her hand on my shoulder and looks me in the eye. "I got you. Now, get in the tub." She helps me step in and then plugs in the clippers. "Ready?" I nod, not because I'm ready but because Farrah doesn't wait for my answer, and when she flips the clippers' switch, they deep-hum and snap, and the bathroom sounds like a bass guitar's been plugged into an amp that's turned up to ten, and nothing bad can come from that sound because that sound is all punk, all possibility. The metal teeth vibrate against my skull. Farrah's fringe sways left to right as she surveys her work. She leans forward and piles my uneven hair on top of my head. She holds my hair with one hand, and her eyes narrow, and then she lets my hair drop to my shoulders.

"Trust me?"

I nod.

She adjusts the clippers and steps behind me into the tub. The clippers groan and struggle as long, thick curls fall into the tub. By the time Farrah flips the switch again, I can't see my feet. She places her hands on each side of my head and rubs, and I feel her hands on both sides of my head. She bobby pins some hair on top of my head as Paul walks in with more eggs. He looks at me and then at Farrah with a big grin. I shrug my shoulders, but his grin tells me something good is happening up there. Paul leans against the wall, opens my notebook, and starts drawing. Farrah steps out of the tub and sips her Tab. "You okay to keep standing?" I nod. She runs her hands through the hair she'd pinned on my head and rubs my scalp. "It only gets better from here."

She cracks egg after egg after egg into the metal bowls, putting the whites in one, the yolks in another, and returning the shells to their cardboard cubbies. Paul looks up from his drawing. "We're turning you into quiche."

"We need tunes," Farrah says.

Paul leaves the notebook on the bathroom sink. He's drawn an egg pushing a giant hair dryer up a hill. I guess that means this will take a while. Farrah cracks the last egg and begins to whisk.

Paul returns with a tape player and a box of tapes and then leaves to cover Farrah's rounds. Farrah points the whisk toward the tapes. "Mute's choice." I flip through the cassettes, choose one, open the tape door with the toe of my hospital slipper, and turn up the volume. Bass guitar thumps through the bathroom. Farrah pops her gum to the beat, separating and pinning what's left of my hair and stepping in and out of the tub to check her work. During her favorite riffs she smacks the tile and tosses her Farrah waves, transforming the bathroom into a CBGB for one. I guess when you look like a Charlie's Angel but rock like a punk, you dance wherever you want. She plugs in the hair dryer and tilts my chin. "Did you think I'd like crap like the Bee Gees?" She squeezes my arm and teases, "Not that there's anything wrong with that. I hear a certain cute boy is into them."

I nod and raise my shoulders, hoping she understands that I don't get how Noah can be so great and yet like such lousy music.

"Boys. They think they're the only ones who can be into bands and know about amps and guitars and shit. Like girls can't read *Melody Maker*."

Farrah could be my new best friend, except she's holding the blow-dryer like a gun, and there's the small fact that my head smells like Bubbe's house when she baked meringues for Passover.

Farrah yells over the hair dryer and the music, "Are you good at makeup and girl crap?"

I shake my head.

"I can show you how to conceal your scar."

She turns off the dryer. "I think it's badass, but boys are chicken-shits when it comes to stuff like that."

She turns the dryer back on, and I curl my toes in my slippers. Stay put, stupid tears. But they don't, because they never do. How do the women on *Woeful Valley* do it? The noise of the blow-dryer can't disguise my wheezes. Farrah notices the wet dots on my hospital gown and turns off the dryer. She wipes my cheeks. "Oh, sweetie. You got it bad for him?"

I nod and hold up ten fingers.

"Ten? Shit."

She steps back and surveys my head. "Well, if he's a ten-finger kind of boy, then the only thing to do is make this big. Really big."

She slaps the tile, rewinds the tape, and turns up the music. Two tapes later her uniform is dark under the arms, and her Farrah feathers are flat. She winds the dryer cord around the handle, tilts my head, and inspects her work. "Your head might feel heavy, but this is some of my best work. You ready?"

I nod.

She pulls her hands away, and my head jerks backward. Farrah steadies it. "Easy, killer. You'll get used to it."

She helps me stand and pulls a hand mirror from her gear bag.

"Close your eyes. No peeking." She positions me in front of the sink mirror. "Ready?"

I nod.

She holds the hand mirror and turns me so I can see myself from all sides. My lip quivers and I try to breathe, but my heart is beating too hard. Farrah looks at me in the mirror. "Oh no. Is it too much?"

I shake my head.

"You like it?"

I've never seen anything like it. My entire head is telling gravity to fuck off. My hair swoops and spikes—a geyser, an explosion, a Mohawk.

#5. Pro: When you stop talking, sometimes people start listening.

I had to sleep sitting up, but it was worth it. During morning rounds the doctors try not to stare, but they're terrible at pretending. Visiting hours don't start until three o'clock, so I spend the afternoon staring at the clock and listening to the beep-beep-beep machine beep faster as two becomes two thirty, two forty-five, and finally three o'clock. I hear the troop clop down the hall. I feel my spikes and pull the sheet up to cover my hospital gown. They rush into my room.

"Frankie!"

"Your hair. Far out!"

"Can I touch it?"

Cliff runs to the bed and plops chocolate kisses, soft from his sweaty palms, onto my lap. He mouth breathes and feels my spikes. "They're so big." Someone snickers, "Like your mama." I scoop the soft chocolates onto the bedside table and try to lean around him. All I see is Cliff, but all I want to see is Noah. Cliff keeps touching my hair. He's had tuna fish for lunch, and it's getting really gross. Finally somebody pulls Cliff's shirt and says, "Man, give her some air." He steps back, and there's my favorite Adventurer standing in the doorway. I can't help the dumb grin on my face as Noah walks toward me. My insides get fluttery and heat rushes to my face and I want to shout as he brushes his tan arm against mine. He smells like cut grass and suntan oil—like the summer that's going on without me, like the buzz of a dial tone that's useless to me now. I want to wrap my arms around his waist and push my cheek into his chest, but no one in the troop knows we're a thing, and while it's de facto acceptable to be a girl in Patriot Adventurers, it's only actually acceptable if everyone in the troop ignores the fact that I'm a girl. If the troop found out the most popular guy *liked me* liked me, they would see me differently and treat me differently, and if everything were different, nothing would be the same, and nothing would work. It works now because the troop treats me just like they treat each other—swirlies and fart jokes.

Noah hooks his pinkie around mine and steps in front of me so no one can see we're holding hands. The beep-beep-beep machine beeps faster, but nobody pays attention because everyone is talking over each other.

"When can you come home?"

"Does it hurt?"

"Do you remember anything?"

"How does your hair stay up?"

I write answers as fast as I can, but I keep forgetting the questions because, when I look at Noah, my brain goes to mush. Mom and George walk out to the hall and Noah leans in and pretends to touch my hair but whispers in my ear, "I wish I could kiss you." Everyone circles the bed and tells me about the subterfuge lessons that I'm missing. They say, "It's not the same without you, it's better." And then, "Ha! Ha!" Noah looks in my eyes without looking away because he knows I'm just pretending to listen. My palms sweat and the beep-beep-beep machine beeps even faster as Noah tap-codes on my leg: M-E-S-S U. I squeeze his hand and start to tap, M-E . . . but George and Mom walk back in. George stands at the foot of the bed, holding a gift-wrapped box.

"Frankie, you brought a voice to Patriot Adventurers we didn't realize we were missing, and when your mother mentioned that you'd been tapping your fingers and she didn't understand why, we knew exactly what you needed."

He raises his hands like a conductor, and the entire troop finds the nearest hard surface, placing their hands on walls, windowsills, doorjambs, and the floor. Noah slips his hand from mine and holds it above the swing-out tray. George snaps his fingers and everyone taps: W-E W-A-N-T T-O H-E-A-R Y-O-U.

The troop must have practiced a ton because everyone taps in unison and no one misspells anything. George passes the box to me, snaps his fingers, and everyone taps: O-P-E-N I-T!

I tear the paper and open the lid, and inside are my favorite sneakers, the red ones with the fat blue laces. George smiles at my confused expression. He snaps again, and everyone taps: T-U-R-N O-V-E-R!

I turn my shoes upside down. There are taps on the bottom of my sneakers! I can tap-code with my feet! If I weren't wearing this stupid backless gown, I'd jump out of bed right now, but instead I slip my hands into the shoes and tap on the swing-out tray: D-Y-N-O-M-I-T-E!

The troop cheers and whoops and crowds the bed, explaining who drilled holes and who came up with the idea. In the clatter Noah walks his fingers up my wrist: C-A-N-T S-T-O-P T-H-I-N-K-I-N-G A-B-O-U . . .

Everyone hangs around the bed, asking questions, and I tap answers with my hands in my new tap shoes, but I'm too fast, so I have to tap everything twice, but I don't care because I've got loud shoes on my hands, and I see a smile on my favorite boy's face. A nurse pokes her head in the door. "Sorry, Frankie. Visiting hours are over. I'm afraid you boys need to leave." I look at the clock and can't believe it's already been an hour. George says, "Okay, troopers, say good-bye." Then he kisses my cheek and steps into the hall to talk with Mom again. The troop files by my bed, and everyone bumps their fists to the taps on my hands. Noah hangs back, and when everyone else is out in the hallway, he reaches into his backpack and pulls out a thin red notebook. Someone from the hall yells, "Hurry up, Fatso" (Noah's nickname because he's thin). Noah yells back, "Shut up." He kisses me and whispers, "Your hair is awesome." And then he walks out the door and joins the rest of the troop. I listen to the elevator doors open. Then the troop packs in, descends, and returns to the freedom of their summer: flip-flops and late-night bike rides, pool parties and pop cans filled with gin.

I open the notebook. On the top of the first page Noah wrote, *Get well soon!* And on the bottom of the page he wrote, *I miss you*, and drew an arrow pointing to the following page. I turn page after page, following the arrows until the last page where he wrote, *this much!!!! Love, Noah.*

Love. He said *love.*

#6. Con: I've never said I love you to a boy.

ESTHER

The sales clerk at the pet store asks so many questions about breed and age that I can't lie fast enough, and I'm so overwhelmed that by the time she asks my dog's name, I blurt out the first thing that comes to mind.

"You named your dog Pepsodent?"

I clench my jaw and nod.

I spend so much money on Frisbees and chew toys that the clerk gives me a free bag of liver snaps and a tennis ball branded with the store's logo. On my way out of the store, I pass a woman pushing a stroller. Her baby teethes on a silver rattle.

In the baby store I try to get away with the cheaper plastic rattle, but the clerk up sells me to sterling silver. She pats my belly, still bloated from my dining room furniture, and asks, "Boy or girl?"

I nod at both and accept free gift wrapping.

On the eleven o'clock news, Chuck reports that the damage to the factory is more significant than previously thought. The factory will be closed the rest of the summer. So for the rest of the night, I alternate between rum, a hot-dog chew toy, liver snaps, and the rattle, but in the end the thing that calms me down is the yellow tennis ball.

When I wake up, anxiety sweats and excessive drool have transferred the Pet Barn's logo on to my swollen cheek and jaw.

RUTH

It's the first day of the Vixen Fixes Your Past! campaign, and I'm in the kitchen when my telephone rings. A panicked voice says, "Mrs. Vixen?"

I hired additional staff in anticipation of an uptick in business, and some of the new employees think my last name is Vixen. It's a daft but not unfounded mistake since the town's other two female businesses are named after their owners, Juliet Pencils and Sherri's Curl Up and Dye.

"This is Ruth."

"The store is packed. People are waiting in long lines. Really long lines."

"I'm sorry. Who is this?"

"It's Adam, from the mall store. People are handing me stuff, and I don't know what to do with it."

"What do you mean, stuff? Do you mean old photographs? That's what the campaign is about."

"Yeah, no. Uh, not exactly."

"Exactly what do you mean then?"

"People are sobbing and handing me stuff. Can you come down here, please?"

"What kind of stuff?"

"There's a woman holding a dictionary and a man holding a cat."

"A live cat?"

"No, it's stuffed."

"Like a stuffed animal?"

"No, like a real cat, but stuffed."

"I'll be there in fifteen minutes."

Traffic is so congested the fifteen-minute drive takes an hour. The tidy white lines of the mall parking lot have been ignored by wood-paneled station wagons triple-parked on the sidewalks. Clumps of people surround the building and Patriot Adventurers pull wagons selling donuts and lemonade.

The crowd assembles without discipline or division. Old men wearing white shoes with black socks stand next to sullen teenagers snapping bubble gum in their overglossed mouths. The teens point and laugh at an old woman whose knee-highs have pooled around her therapeutic shoes. Crying people stand next to laughing people, both eyeing each other in disbelief. Everyone is carrying something. A woman with a triangle-folded American flag stands next to a man holding a framed photograph. His photo isn't in a bag or protective box, and it looks like he pulled the picture off the wall and came straight to the mall without bothering to dust it.

At the back of the mall, there are even more people, and they're blocking the employee entrance. I point to my Vixen nametag, and a man shaking a torn stuffed bunny over his head helps me push open the heavy mall door. Inside I push and "Please" and "Excuse me," but the crowd is so loud that no one hears me, so I just shove through the people until I see the food court manager selling hot pretzels.

"What's going on?" I ask.

I'm close enough to smell the manager's mouthwash, but I have to yell so he can hear me.

"It's your idea, right?" he says.

"My idea?"

"To fix people's past."

"Fixing people's past? What are you talking about?"

"The campaign."

"The campaign is about repairing old photos . . ."

"Repairing memories, yeah. Brilliant idea, Ruth. Who doesn't want a do-over?"

"That isn't what I meant. I meant fixing old images, like pictures faded from—"

"People always said you were cranky, but man, you're really tuned in. These people camped out overnight."

"Overnight?"

"You want a hot pretzel?"

I shake my head, then jostle and bump through the throngs until I reach the door concealed in the vixen's tail. I climb inside her haunch and pull her big paw to shut the door. The kid working the front counter turns around. His nametag reads "Adam."

"Hi, Adam. I'm Ruth." I point to the vixen's head. "Close her eyes and come back here, please."

The customer service windows are the vixen's eyes. Adam closes the metal shutters, and the din of the crowd muffles. I step over a decanter of whiskey, a bulging pile of legal-size folders, and what looks like a birthday cake.

"Is that a cake?" I ask.

"Yeah."

"How long has it been like this?"

"The cake?"

"No, not the cake"—I motion with my hands—"all of this, the people."

"When I got here, it was already like this, Mrs. Vixen. I heard people started arriving last night. Did you see the bus?"

"What have you been telling people?"

"I've been taking their stuff and making them fill out development envelopes with their name and address, and then I tear off the tabs from the envelopes and give it to the customer, just like normal. I didn't know what else to do. When I got here, there was already a line around the mall."

I reach for my Vixen apron.

"This is a simple misunderstanding; I'm sure we can clear this up."

He looks me in the eye, rare for a teenage boy.

"I tried explaining, but no one listened."

"Thank you. You've done the right thing. I'm sure they'll listen to me."

I tighten my apron and put my hand on his back.

"Ready?"

We each lift an eyelid, and the swarming crowd cheers. I lean out and greet the first customer.

"Welcome to Vixen."

A woman stands on her tiptoes and thrusts a man's blue dress shirt in my face.

"Smell it," she says.

"I'd rather not. Can I help you with your film or printing needs?"

"This isn't my perfume"—she turns up the collar—"and this isn't my lipstick." She points to her lips and then to the shirt collar and then back to her lips. "I wear red, this is pink. Fix it." I keep my hands at my side, and the shirt hangs between us, a button-down accusation.

"I'm sorry. I think there's been a mistake. The only thing I can fix is . . ."

She shakes the shirt. "You promised to fix the past."

"I can fix old images, not dress shirts. Do you have a photograph I can repair? Perhaps an image that's faded from the sun because you left it on the back of your piano?"

"I don't have a piano. Not anymore." She rocks from toe to heel. "You're useless."

I reach under the counter. "A few coupons?"

She looks at the coupons and then at me. "There's shit in your hair."

She turns, and the crowd reabsorbs her until she's just an arm, thrust skyward, clutching a blue shirt. I run my fingers through my hair, and a tuft of stuffed bunny falls on the counter. Adam pulls a mailman's bag through the small window, and it flops over the counter and thuds on the floor. He turns to me. "He steamed open the letters, he read things he shouldn't . . ."

I nod. "Give him an order number and some two-for-one coupons."

"What do I put on the order envelope?" he asks.

I don't know because this isn't what I meant. This isn't why I rented billboards and bought full-page ads. This isn't a fix. The explosion was bad, but this is worse because we've ignored the inherent contract of the Midwest: shove it down, suffer in private, and then get on with life. Maybe I can run another ad? Explain to all these people who camped out overnight that *I'm sorry but you've misunderstood*. I turn away and take a deep breath. I'm alive.

I return to the crowd, force a smile, and motion for the next customer to step up onto the platform.

"Welcome to Vixen. What can I fix?"

A gray-haired tailor explains he wanted his wife to lose weight, but she wouldn't give up sweets, so once a week he took in the waistband of her pants.

"I altered at night, while she slept."

"Did it work?"

"Yes."

"So, how can I help you?"

"She dropped the weight, and then she dropped me."

I pass him an envelope, and he pulls eyeglasses from his shirt pocket and begins to fill in his information. When he's finished, he heaves an industrial sewing machine onto the counter. Behind him, a teenage boy tosses a tennis ball in the air and pretends to hit it with an invisible tennis racket, catching the ball before it bounces. I tear the tab off the tailor's envelope and hand it to him with a nod. I try to move the sewing machine to the floor but it's too heavy, so it stays on the counter. The tailor walks away as the tennis player shoves the ball up the leg of his shorts and steps to the window. Two bracelets of braided and multicolored thread circle his left arm. They're bloated and faded as if he's never removed them, not for a shower, not for a swim in the lake. I think the kids call these friendship bracelets, because every summer when they return from camp and drop off a summer's worth of film, begging, *Triple prints, please!* their arms are stacked with these thready declarations.

"How can I help you?" I ask.

He looks down at his shoes. "I took something."

His voice is deeper than his baby face suggests.

"You stole something?"

"Kinda?"

I look at his forearm and his blond hair. I glance at the crowd. Teen girls fluff their hair and angle their breast buds in his direction.

"Can you return it?" I ask.

"It's . . . um . . . the kind of thing you can't return. I thought I wanted it, but then I realized I didn't."

I look at his face and try to remember what it's like to be young, when small mistakes feel like eternal consequences. I stifle the instinct to dismiss him—*Believe me, it gets worse with age*—and instead I think about things that can be taken but not returned. I hand him a developing envelope. "Fill this out. In the special instructions box, put a name. I'll see what I can do, but I think you're the only one that can fix this." Then I lean forward. "Just call her."

He fills out the form in big awkward letters. How am I going to get through all these people? I glance at Adam, and he's holding a pipe wrench and a pair of ripped women's pantyhose. I place the tennis player's form on the pile.

A woman with toothpick arms and limp hair thuds a big dictionary onto the counter. "I want you to fix this." A miasma of mildew and stale cooking oil surrounds her.

"Is there something wrong with your dictionary?" I ask.

"It's not the dictionary. It's the things I've said. I want to take them back."

"You want to take back all the things you've ever said?"

"No, just the things I said to my mother," she says. "I've underlined all the words."

I slide an order form across the counter, and she grabs my hand. I pull out from under her and put my hand in my apron pocket. I know that ache, the desperate need for the reprieve of skin on skin, but I can't. Not today. If I soften, I'll dissolve. I tear the tab off her envelope and slide it across the counter and move the dictionary to the floor, then say, "Next customer, please."

For hours I accept positive biopsies, negative pregnancy tests, and sketchbooks from engineers who wished they were painters. Accountants surrender ledgers and confess to cooking the uncooked books and uncooking the cooked books, and none of it makes sense, but all of it kills my appetite. I instruct customers to fill out the developing envelopes completely and specifically, and when they return the forms, I treat them like any other film order, tearing off the top tab, handing it to them as a receipt, and saying, "We'll contact you when your order is finished."

I charge everyone the same amount, except for the dentist. The hairdresser who dumps a wad of hair on the counter and confesses he told his clients they looked good even when they didn't, "especially when they didn't," pays the same as the doctor who amputated the wrong leg. But when the dentist with gambling debts bites his lip and mumbles about using paper clips instead of dental steel, I charge him triple. Distress varies by profession and age, but men are as simple and as complicated as women, and fathers are less vocal but just as aggrieved as mothers, a realization that displeases the mothers and leaves them cross-armed and resentful. Women in their late twenties regret abandoning their girlfriends for boyfriends, and women in their thirties regret abandoning everything for the demands of their children, husbands, and homes. With slumped shoulders and thick middles, they ask, "Is it supposed to be this hard?"

Misery mounts itself: High school yearbooks stack on top of wedding albums that pile on top of one cracked swimming fin, a jelly jar filled with pink sand labeled "Honeymoon 1953." A tuba, engineering schematics for tunnels, X-rays of wrist bones, and a manila envelope filled with something that shakes like flour and is labeled with duct tape: "Dad."

A toothbrush with stained bristles, a couch pillow, a welcome-home doormat—I learn to look beyond the objects that people hand me, because suffering is tricky to articulate, and a thing is easier than a feeling. It's easier to grab a thing and shove it in a bag, hurl it on a counter, and say, *Fix this.* People do bring photographs, framed and unframed, wallet size and glossy photo-booth strips, but after nine hours, when someone approaches the counter asking for repaired corners or improved color, I wonder what they're hiding, and if I stand still long enough, their lips quiver, and they give in, holding up their photographs and saying, "I want to be like this again" or "I never want to be like that again." Every recipe tin, bad wig, and spelling bee trophy is labeled and tagged, and when we run out of space, Adam commandeers the food court, and when the food court tables are full, we pile things on the mall floor as if the furry vixen is hosting a yard sale for the disillusioned and aggrieved.

ESTHER

I'm lying on the couch, watching *Woeful Valley*, pressing a bag of frozen peas against my swollen Pet Barn–logo jaw. Sarah is in the courtroom defending her twin sister, Lucy, who's accused of robbing a bank, but Lucy didn't rob the bank, Sarah's husband did. Sarah is torn between her big love and her twin sister because she doesn't know that Lucas was the one who hit her with the drainpipe and put her in a coma so that he could dress as Lucy and commit crimes because he's in love with Lucy, not Sarah. Sarah grasps her IV pole and bangs her fist on the table and yells, "Objection, Your Honor. Hearsay."

"Yeah! Take that." I pump the bag of frozen peas in the air and pea sweat drips on my forehead as the special news bulletin chimes. Anchorman Chuck is live at the mall, interviewing people who are trying to fix their past. Must be nice to believe that anything at the mall could fix your life. My problem isn't my past, my problem is my future and my very oozing present because the tennis ball logo gave me mouth sores. I throw the peas in the garbage and pull a cold Tab from the fridge and hold it against my face. I stare out my kitchen window. Cute Guy's Monte Carlo isn't in his parking spot. The TV says something about gridlocked traffic at the mall. No way I'm going to the mall, but a walk would do me good.

I end up at the Craft Barn on the south end of town. I browse through rows of macramé supplies and googly eyes; the clerk assures me that jigsaw puzzles and knitting can solve any problem.

"Even my problem?"

"Yes. Any problem."

I buy a 1000 piece puzzle of a horse standing in a field of flowers. I also buy knitting needles and some yarn to knit Frankie a poncho. I don't know how to knit, but now seems like a good time to start. I walk home a different way and pass carloads of people waiting to turn in to the mall. I shove horse hooves and daisy petals in my mouth. The puzzle pieces are depressing; they bloat and soften too fast, and for the rest of the walk, I spit horse and daisy into people's shrubs. By the time I reach my apartment, the puzzle box is empty.

Cute Guy's Monte Carlo still isn't in the parking lot, so I kill time, walking around the scrubby field, hoping he'll show up. I imagine him pulling into the parking lot and jumping out of the driver's side while his dog jumps out of the passenger side. Cute Guy tosses a Frisbee into the field, and his dog runs after it, but I can run faster than the dog, and I look cute chasing a Frisbee; my hair blows in the wind as I leap and catch the disc one-handed. Cute Guy's dog wags his tail and bounds over to lick me, and Cute Guy will be so impressed with my Frisbee skills that he'll ask me over to his apartment for a beer, and then we'll go on a date, and our first date will be so great there will be more dates, and those dates will be so great that we'll move in together, and then we'll get married, and Cute Dog will have puppies, and we'll live happily ever after.

After an hour of looping the scrubby field, my stomach is cramping, and I think I might vomit. I throw the puzzle box in the trash and check my mailbox; nothing good, just bills I can't pay because I don't have a job anymore.

I lie on the couch and stare at the knitting needles and the yarn. What if I forget how to do my job? It's been weeks since I've bitten anything with precision. The puzzle pieces had novel shapes, but in the end, they were all surface and no substance. I miss pencils. Pencils have structural integrity, and they don't give me painful gas. A commercial for scented tampons comes on television, another woman running in a field, feeling daisy fresh. The male voice-over says, "You think you don't need scented tampons, but you do."

Shut up.

I grab the bottle of rum off the coffee table. Tomorrow, I'll knit.

FRANKIE

My future hinges on one word: *but.*

I read my chart. When the ambulance brought me in, the surgeons were more concerned about my heart than my throat. They worried that the pencil shards bobbing in my bloodstream could prick my heart and beat, blam, splat, no more me, so they prioritized the extraction of all the pencil fragments and didn't worry too much about potential damage to my vocal cords. I'm no doctor, and after my time in here I don't ever want to be one, but I get it, it's a hard choice, and they made the choice most adults would—that it's more important to be alive than to be talkative. The post-op surgery notes say, *Acute penetrative laryngeal trauma. Complete fragment removal unconfirmed. Significant penetrative injuries. Speech recovery possible, but unlikely.* Any normal person would understand two things. Thing one: the word after *but* is the truth. Speech recovery possible, but *unlikely.* Thing two: all the words before *but* are pie in the sky, dream on, fat chance. But my mother is not normal, she's a Rosenblum, and when she heard *possible, but unlikely,* she ignored the *but unlikely* and focused on the *possible* because her entire life has been about making the unlikely possible. But yesterday, unlikely became impossible.

Mom demanded a specialist, and the specialist was specialized enough to maintain a neutral face while she examined me, but when she stepped into the hall to talk with Mom, her expression was tight-lipped, then Mom broke down and Rosenblum-sobbed. No one tells me what's happening, but it doesn't matter. I might have missed the subterfuge lesson in Patriot Adventurers, but the faces of all the doctors and nurses, therapists and specialists, speak loudly enough, and what they're saying is: I'll never talk again.

And just like that, I'm a mute.

This morning the fifth-floor crazy doctor showed up. She handed me a stack of flashcards, black-and-white drawings of circle-head faces with oval eyes and mouths that are either right-side-up arcs or upside-down arcs. Real heady stuff. Dr. Crazy stood at the foot of my bed and asked complicated questions but expected circle-head answers.

"How do you feel about not speaking?"

"How do you feel about your pain?"

"Have you had your menses?"

"What do you think about your mother?"

Smiley face.

Smiley face.

Frown face.

Smiley face.

She gathered the cards and snapped the brass locks of her briefcase and said, "You're either very well adjusted or an excellent liar."

I pulled the pencil from my Mohawk and underneath a smiley face wrote: *Same diff.*

Later in the middle of the night, Paul wraps the rubber band around my arm and starts to Nosferatu my blood.

"Hey, sunshine," he says.

Blood flows into the vial as he tilts his head toward Noah's Bee Gees T-shirt that I slept in.

"This is a single room, missy. Cavorting with your boyfriend is against hospital policy."

He lifts the sheets and pretends to look for Noah, and it's kind of funny, so I start smiling, but before I even realize what's happening,

I'm shaking and heaving and doing my new weird silent-movie cry, all scrunched face without the normal sound track of sucking snot and heaving waaaaahs.

"Hey, are you okay? Did I hit a nerve?"

I shake my head.

"Hang in there, I'm almost done."

He presses a cotton ball against my arm, moves the blanket out of the way, and plops onto the bed, wrapping his arm around my shoulder. "Okay. It can't be your hair because that looks amazing. So what is it?" I open my notebook to the *Pro/Con Stab* list. Paul reads it and then closes the notebook. He leans back, resting his head in his hands. We stare at the empty ceiling. The balloons deflated a while ago.

Paul shoots my tissue wads into the trash can underneath the TV. Most of them miss, but the last one swoops into the can, and Paul pumps his fist. The bed shakes.

Paul hands me a tissue, and while I blow, he leaves out his hand to take it back, but I shake my head and shoot it myself. It lands on the floor, miles away from the can.

"Ever heard of John Cage?"

I shake my head.

"He's a composer who's so into silence that he once hung out in a soundproof chamber. And you know what he heard in that space where you aren't supposed to hear anything? He heard his body, his circulatory system, his nervous system. That's crazy, right? There is no silence, even in a fancy room that's supposed to be quiet."

I throw another tissue. Another miss.

"Sunshine, silence is impossible. You're making noise all the time. Your blood cells, your hormones, it's just that most people can't hear anything other than the sound of their own voice."

Paul balls fresh tissues from the box and shoots four baskets that all go in. "Just because you can't talk doesn't mean you don't have stuff to say."

He stands up, gathers the blood vials, and writes notes in my chart. "Besides, not every boy gives up his favorite band T-shirt."

Thinking about how cute Noah is and what a hole-in-the-neck-virgin I am makes me tear up again. Paul squeezes my foot. "Mutey Rosenblum, listen up. Number one, the tissue box is empty, so you're going to have to stop crying. And number two, you have a gigantic wave on your head held together with egg whites and love. You're a punk, and punks don't give a shit about the obvious and the expected, and what's more obvious than talking with your mouth?"

Paul pushes his cart toward the door and out into the hall. I wipe my nose on the sheet and begin counting ceiling tiles. I'm on number twenty-five when Paul pops his head back in. "Go make some noise."

I count the entire ceiling twenty times, and then around four a.m. I get up and lace my new tap-code sneakers. I walk to the foot of my bed and introduce old me to new me.

My right foot says, H-E-L-L-O?

My left foot says, H-I.

My right foot asks, F-R-A-N-K-I-E?

My left foot answers, Y-E-P I-T-S M-E.

I say my name. First fast and then slow, emphasizing the *F* and then the *e*.

I walk into the tiny bathroom. The tile floor and walls amplify my voice. I step into the shower, more echoes but better reverb. I shout my name without moving my lips. I'm rolling thunder and summer hail: pellet and pound. I pick up my hairbrush, and my feet sing. I'm a stack of Marshall amps, Iggy Pop, and the Stooges. I'm a riot of one.

I don't want to stop.

The linoleum hallway swallows my words in late-night hospital hush-hush. Open doors expand my speech and closed doors reject it, saying, *Take-it-back, take-it-back.* Patients sit up and stare and point at me, the girl with singing shoes. I've walked my entire life, but now I'm a soliloquy, metallic and in motion.

In the concrete stairwell my thoughts overlap and stutter, down two flights and back up one, all jangle and ring. With each rise and fall, I rule my cement kingdom. In the elevator I'm high-pitched and chatty; I lean back and let my feet push the buttons. The chapel has rich wooden floors, and the landing strip on either side of the pews is a carpet of confessions. I stand at the front of the room and preach, all jubilant and Glory Be. I'm the soloist and the choir: piano, tambourine, and clap, clap. Amen.

In the waiting area for the emergency room, I'm muffled and anxious like everyone else. The carpet is stained and the magazines are old. Everyone is waiting for good news, but I'm so tired of waiting. I can't do it. Not anymore. It's time to make my own news. I get up and run as fast as a girl and her IV pole can, and when I reach the padded mat in front of the big glass doors, I swing my foot, and the door swooshes open, and I'm outside for the first time in way too long. Summer blows her muggy breath on my face. I talk with cement ribbon sidewalks and tap benedictions when the ambulances rush in. I cross the parking lot, joking with rubbery tires and arguing with chrome bumpers. On sloping speed bumps and against angular curbs, I listen to my blasting timbre and blooming tone. The moon is fat and bright.

I prop my feet against an oak tree. He's a good listener. My words vibrate through his bark and rumble into his trunk. They thread around his thick roots, winding down, down, into the earth, where worms escort my sentences through water and soil, beyond microbes and paused rain, past the earth's mantle, until they reach her core, where they jump and swirl in hot magma. It's so late that it's early. Not a car door, not a cricket, but even in this silence, there's noise, because way down in the raucous fire-heart of the earth is a punk band, and I just became its singer.

The first person I tell is Paul, and Paul helps me tell the second person.

"Hi, Noah. This is Nurse Paul from Lead General. No, there's nothing wrong. She's okay, she just wants to talk to you."

Paul gives me the phone and goes out into the hall so I can have privacy. He's good that way. He doesn't know tap code, but he pretends it's the same as talking.

"Hi."

H-I.

"Miss me as much as I miss you?"

N-O.

There's silence on the other end. Noah swallows, and I hear his mouth open, but before he can speak, I tap, M-O-R-E.

He sighs.

"The moon is boring without you."

Y-O-U W-A-N-N-A M-O-O-N M-E?

It's hard to explain how I feel. I'm the same, but I'm not; I'll never be the same. It's a lot to tap with my fingers, but Noah gets it. We stay on the phone most of the night, and when he asks me about the sky, I squint and tell him the lights of the beep-beep-beep machine look just like stars.

RUTH

The mall smells like hot mustard and flat pop. Mascara-fresh faces are long gone; it's nothing but raccoon eyes and flaking lips. Everyone's clothes are slept in and hot-pretzel stained. Sharp-shaven faces have reverted to cave-dwelling countenances. A group of school children braided all the men's neckties into a rope they use to double Dutch. I've closed the other two Vixen locations because the mall is the only space big enough to hold everyone and everything.

My experiments in domesticity generally failed, but Max was a good sport. He ate lumpy mashed potatoes with a smile and shuffled around the house in crocheted slippers four sizes too big. He wore my lousy handicrafts and ate my globby food, saying, *Not bad for a chimp.* It was his catchall phrase because, as much as we like to imagine otherwise, we're nothing but animals, nothing but apes. Maybe he meant it as a joke, but I took it seriously. We cufflink and pantyhose to mask our animal nature, but it's only when someone's animal emerges that you see their true self, and after nights of sleeping on food court tables and brushing their teeth while looking at pennies in the mall fountain, everyone's animal is surfacing.

The factory workers don't have the luxury of dwelling in the past because the lousy present clings to them like the graphite cloud hanging over the factory. The first man in line wears a jumpsuit the color of moss, and before I can say anything, he reaches for my hand. "How are you?"

How am I? I have no idea. I say, "I'm thirsty," because I am.

"Aren't we all," he says.

A fresh burn, pink and raw, licks his face.

He squeezes my hand tighter and says, "Your eyes are beautiful. They're gray, like fog."

I flinch and close my eyes. Max described my eyes as fog rolling across a Nordic fjord. The first time he said it, I thought it was the most ridiculous thing I'd ever heard. I mocked him and said, *As if you've ever seen a Nordic fjord.* Max's fjord compliment became our lifelong joke. After sex I'd roll over, look in his eyes, and tease, *Swedish fjord? Alaskan fjord?* When I exhausted all the oceans and seas that have fjords, I switched to the fjord-free Great Lakes and domestic rivers. *Superior? Mississippi? Big Muddy?* I memorized tributaries and streams. The morning he died, I rolled over and asked, *Quinnipiac?* He held my face and said, *You don't get it. It's not the fjord, it's the fog, the rolling energy that mesmerizes and transforms, it makes you lose your bearings.*

I open my eyes. I've gone too long without speaking. "Welcome to Vixen. What can I fix?"

"I was next to the graphite vat when it exploded."

Bits of graphite are burned into his raw skin. I don't know what to say, so I slide an envelope toward him.

"Do you have anything larger?"

He's not holding anything, but I say, "Yes, for special orders. Would you like that?"

He nods.

I lean under the counter to get a big envelope, and when I stand, I'm eye level with his naked chest, red wounds where hair used to be, and the beginning of a zipper-teeth scab. He pulls his arms from his jumpsuit sleeves. "Thank you," he says, taking the envelope. He pulls the zipper over ribs, over his skin that's stretched tight and oozing, an interior breaching its exterior. An elderly woman in Adam's line shields her eyes with her pocketbook. The naked and burned man holds his jumpsuit at arm's length, bringing one shoulder to meet the other, folding it in half and then half again until the jumpsuit slides into the envelope. He closes his eyes and inhales. His neck veins bulge, and his ribs accordion, and then he exhales into the envelope, licks the seal, and slides it to me.

"I felt the heat, and I inhaled the graphite. My lungs are scarred, and the doctor said the smell might never go away, that I might always smell smoke when I breathe. I worked double shifts and overtime. For what?" He taps the envelope, then turns around, and walks through the crowd to the food court. He steps into the fountain and sits cross-legged, but the shallow water can't cover his nakedness. Wading toddlers splash and squeal, and he smiles and reaches out, but their mothers snatch them before he can touch their chubby fingers. He reaches into the water and pulls out the blue button-down shirt with the lipstick on the collar that the woman tried to give me a few days ago. He wrings it out, wraps it around his waist, and sits on the edge of the fountain. Older kids pelt him with pennies, but he just smiles and tries to catch them.

After hours and hours of collecting the past and tearing off the perforated tabs of the future, I ask the mall manager to hang the **CLOSED** sign on the mall door. He barely understands me because my voice is so hoarse. I call in favors. The owner of the camping store delivers tents and sleeping bags. People pitch tents and eat hot pretzels for dinner, happy to have some privacy. Adam passes out numbers to the crowd still waiting outside. He explains they can go home and return tomorrow, and their place in line will be guaranteed, but no one leaves.

I send Adam home and shut the vixen's eyes. I shove binders of crop forecasts, step over a stack of draft cards, and crush a glass shadowbox of unworn baby booties. I grab one of the many flasks; this one is silver and has a cap shaped like a golf ball. The back is scratched from years of brushing against car keys and pocket change. The bottom is inscribed, *To NGE, my favorite hole in one.* I shut myself in the camera obscura and unscrew the golf ball.

After some deep swallows, my breathing slows, and my eyes adjust to the darkness of the camera obscura. On the ceiling, the food court fountain shimmers with the cheap currency of sunken desires and wads of gum. Discarded pop cans and hot-pretzel wrappers bob in the water. I know the water isn't on the ceiling, but I close my eyes anyway, hoping it will slip down my throat and wash away this day.

ESTHER

Knit-one and purl-two is cross-eyed bullshit. The shiny needles are the perfect size and hardness, but the frosted metal makes my filings zing, so all I can do is unwind and rewind the yarn around my arm until my fingers turn blue. Maybe I should clean my house. The women in commercials are happy after they clean their houses. I wrap a kerchief around my head to make it official, and then I wash and dust and straighten and fold and fluff. I put a sock on my hand and clean my blinds and then sock all the nooks and crannies in my apartment. I open my closet and pull the bitten wooden hangers off the rod and throw them into a thick black garbage bag. On top of the hangers I toss all the chew toys, gnawed plungers, and the store-logo tennis ball that gave me mouth sores. I drag everything down the stairs to the basement trash room.

It smells like stale beer and bloated cardboard down here. I open the small incinerator door and heave the heavy bag, but the door is small and my bag is big. A plunger handle pokes through the plastic, and the bag tears, and the eviscerated, yet somehow still squeaking, hot-dog chew toy rolls across the floor.

"They bite through those things fast, don't they?"

The cute Monte Carlo–driving, Frisbee-throwing, strong-chomper-dog-owning guy is standing in the doorway, balancing an empty pizza box on his hip. I shove my bag harder into the tiny chute, hoping to burn what is a big bag of crazy before he gets close enough to wonder why I'm burning a closet's worth of hangers and more toilet plungers than a healthy person needs. The bag rips further, and a plunger thwacks onto the floor. I shove it with my foot and hope he doesn't notice, but of course he notices because toilet plungers are that thing that everyone notices even when they pretend they don't. But for some reason he keeps walking until he is standing next to me. He holds open the incinerator door with his tanned, muscled arm, and he gives my bag the last push it needs. Red plunger tops glow in the fire, and I block his view by wedging my body between the incinerator and his arm.

"What kind of dog do you have?" he asks.

Out of the corner of my eye, I see a plunger melt in the flames. I hope he doesn't think I'm the one that smells like burning rubber. I turn my shoulders a bit more to block the flaming plungers, and darn, this door is hot.

"That hot-dog toy, it's for a dog, right?"

I laugh. "Of course. Yes. My dog? Oh, uh, he's a mutt."

"Mine's a mutt too."

"Mutts, yeah, they're the best. I like all kinds of mutts, dog mutts, cat mutts, pizza mutts . . ."

"You mind?"

He leans forward. Do I have something on my face? I touch my face and see that I'm still wearing a yellow rubber glove on one hand and a sock on the other and, oh crap, my hair is in the stupid kerchief. I smile, and my eyes bug out, and why is he asking if I mind . . .

"I need to throw this away."

"Of course, I mean why else would you be in the trash room. I mean it's not like I hang out in here or anything . . ."

He laughs, and I try to step out of the way, but I trip on the plunger and lurch forward and grab his arm with my sock hand.

"Most people put their socks on the other end," he says.

I smile and shrug my shoulders.

He laughs. "You okay?"

I'm so far from okay that I need a passport to travel there. Deep breath, push that way, way down because one day I will be one of those women, the ones who wear white pants on their period and run through fields of daisies. The cute Monte Carlo–driving, Frisbee-throwing guy slides his pizza box into the fire as if it's the simplest thing in this dumb, hard world.

"What's a pizza mutt?"

I'd forgotten I said that. "A pizza with everything on it? Bit of this, bit of that . . ."

He closes the incinerator door and looks me up and down. "You're funny. I've never heard it described that way, but you're right."

I put my sock hand on my hip and tilt my head toward the trash chute. "So, was that a pizza mutt?"

We talk about pizza, and then we talk about dogs, and I'm so happy that we aren't talking about plungers that when he tells me his dog loves to play Frisbee, I pretend I don't already know, which is an easy lie since I'm already lying about owning a dog. I pretend to listen, but I'm thinking of all my coworkers who (a) have dogs, (b) would let me borrow their dogs, and (c) have a dog that would pretend to know and like me because there's something really wrong if your own dog doesn't like you; and (d) do I have a good side and (e) is it my left or right? I can't remember, so I pivot, and he asks if I'm a ballet dancer. I laugh and rise on my toes, turn, and nearly fall against the incinerator door, but his ropey arms reach out and steady me, so I kick my leg and shout, "Disco. I dance disco!" His Foghat T-shirt pulls tight across his chest, and he laughs and twirls me in the trash room as my plunger caps smolder in shame.

The cute Monte Carlo–driving, Frisbee-throwing guy tells me his name is Brad. He lives two floors above me, and next Friday we have a date.

Ruth

The campaign ended yesterday. I'm exhausted, but I can't sleep because people's tchotchkes have commandeered my dreams. The owner of the mall wants his space back, so I've got to figure out where to move the parade of regret.

I call the mother superior at St. Lucy's Academy and ask about renting the gym.

"Only the Lord can lighten people's burdens," she says.

"That's not what you said after waiting in line to give me your accounting ledgers," I remind her.

After a hefty payment that she insists on calling a donation, I secure the gym for the next thirty days, all the time available before the school year begins. I call a moving company, and after I write another check, they transport a truckload of misery from the mall to the gym at St. Lucy's Academy, where Frankie may or may not be able to return to school. I arrange for a ladder and tables, and when the last box is unloaded and the truck pulls away, it's just me, a thermos of coffee, two tuna fish sandwiches, and boxes stacked twenty high, filling the gym from foul line to foul line. The movers left thin alleyways between the rows of boxes, and to navigate them, I have to turn sideways and suck in my stomach.

For days I leaned out of the vixen's eyes and assumed that when the mayhem ended I would know what to do, but now it's over, and

I don't have a clue. Why did I think boxes and order numbers would translate the Sisyphean into the surmountable? I climb the bleachers and walk around the gym, hoping for perspective, but none appears. So I start tearing strips of duct tape with my teeth. The ripping sound pings off the cement block walls. I use the tape to divide the bleachers into many small sections. My lips taste like adhesive, but after a few hours the left side of the gym is partitioned. I drag a ladder to a stack under the visitor's hoop and climb until I reach the top box. I lift it off and carry it to the top row of bleachers, and now that the box is here, there's nothing to do but surrender to the rhythm of reaching in and pulling out, palming the weight of everyone's past.

Order #469 is a hand-knit sweater with one arm longer than the other. Underneath that sweater is order #1507, a chip of a ruby that's wrapped in a dusty tissue. In the same box is the dictionary submitted by the thin woman who smelled like mildew and cooking oil. On almost every page, words are circled or underlined. When she stood in front of me, her voice was so quiet, but this is quite the effort, hauling a verbose past into her silent future. Underneath the dictionary is order #382, a framed snapshot of shiny packages under a tinseled Christmas tree. Next to the tree is a round coffee table with a glass of milk and a plate of cookies. The description on the developing envelope says, *Christmas was ruined.* The tree is big and green and ribboned with glowing lights. The cookies look homemade, and there are four stockings hanging over the mantel. Are you remembering this right? There are cookies and colored lights. How bad could it have been? It was only one moment, but for someone, and for some reason, that moment has eclipsed all the moments that came before or after.

"Ruth?"

I hadn't realized the gym had grown dark until Sam flips on the lights.

"Up here." I wave from the top row of bleachers. I place a box of recipe cards next to a large clump of brown human hair. Sam puts his camera bag on the gym floor and climbs until he's at the end of my row. I pat the empty section of bleacher.

"What is that?"

"Hair. I think."

"Disgusting."

"Not as disgusting as the dentures."

"Someone gave you old teeth?"

"Several people have given me old teeth. One person gave me a tooth."

Sam thumbs through the recipe cards.

"I thought once I could see it all, I'd know what to do, but now that it's all out, all I want to do is just pack it back up."

Sam steps into the next row and picks up the stuffed bunny that loses stuffing every time it's touched. "Light it on fire?"

We laugh until we realize what we've said.

"The light in here blows," he says.

I nod.

"I brought you food. Figured you could use some dinner."

"I could use something."

"Well, here's a cheeseburger."

"Fries?"

"Always."

We eat and stare across the gym at the bleachers. I hear myself chewing pickle and swallowing hamburger bun. I hate that. Tomorrow, I'll bring a radio.

Sam tilts his chocolate malt in my direction, but I shake my head.

"How long do you think this will take?" he asks.

I rub a fry in the salt at the bottom of the bag. "I have no idea."

Sam finishes his malt, then squeezes my shoulders, gathers the food wrappers, and promises to check in soon. As he leaves, his boots echo against the empty lockers in the hall.

For days, I drive home, barely sleep, and return to the gym to unpack the stuff of sadness and misunderstanding. The lonesome architecture of a ring missing its jewel, a strand of long red hair, a poorly folded roadmap, and a gold-capped human incisor, rootless and stunned. Five Little League trophies with scratched-out nameplates. A large woman's winter coat with two pin holes over the breast as if she favored a heavy broach, a half dozen *World's Best Dad!* mugs, most of them chipped and coffee stained, but one with insides so white it either was never given or never used. There's so much paper: birth certificates, report cards, wills, unfinished theses, to-do lists, house inspections, tax returns, banking ledgers, love letters, hate letters, and registered letters. My fingers are thrashed stalks. I call the office supply store, and they deliver a pallet of envelopes, and into their yellow mouths, I slide medical charts, unsigned Mother's Day cards, wedding invitations, and World War II telegrams that flake into my lap. *I'm coming home. Stop.* Or, *We're sorry to inform you that Nick won't be coming home. Stop.*

On the fifth day I unroll a drawing of a claw-foot bathtub surrounded by electrical appliances that are organized by cord length. The coffeepot is crossed out with the notation *Cord too short.* Underneath the mixer, *Too heavy to lift while in tub.* The blender is *too slippery*, but the toaster is circled in red pen, *Cord length accommodates immersion.* The drawing is beautiful, but there's something unsettling in the exact detail of the cords and plugs, and maybe that's why I start crying, but I doubt it. I lie on the floor and look up at the high ceiling, at the volleyball championship banners and the caged lights. The widow who, for days, hasn't spoken to anything but her teapot. "I could use some help."

Max was a scientist. He solved equations and discerned patterns, throwing the anchor of his life into deep space and asking: What about this? What about that? By the time we found each other, we'd already been lost with other lovers, so on the night when my dress pooled emerald around my ankles, I slid between the sheets tarnished by previous men. It's not that I didn't shine, I did. I was polished; I was ready, but I diffused my own light because I'd already learned that men fear the refulgent. A woman shines, and men are frightened by their own shadows. But that night, I realized I was wrong; he was different, he kept his eyes open and he sighed, *Brilliant.* And from that night on, we built a life of shared luminosity, neither existing in the other's shadow.

On our honeymoon, Max convinced me that it was only the weight of his hands, pressed into my shoulders, that kept me from floating off the bed, transitioning from particle to wave. *There's too much gravity,* he said. *More than makes sense, more than we need.* When I asked him what he meant, he explained that science only understands a sliver of the universe, but one thing scientists have figured out is there's more gravity than makes sense. I didn't understand the logic of that until right now, as I orbit from foul line to foul line, propelled by the gravity of miscommunication.

The light in the gym is windowless and without valor, not even enough courage to cast a decent shadow. I go home; I come back; I go home again.

Order #51 and order #253, two identical gold charm bracelets, one with a dangling *M* charm, the other with a dangling *R*. Both envelopes say the bracelet was a gift from *my mother*, and judging by the order numbers, the sisters arrived on different days, and while they may or may not have been aware of each other's visit, they both wrote the same thing in the special instructions box: *Mom loved her more than me.* I hold one bracelet in each palm. Of course she loved one of you more. Love isn't equal, love isn't cake, you can't sift, measure, and then level the top of the cup with the flat side of a knife. I put the gold circles back on the bleacher and stare up at the hateful caged lights. Delusions of uniqueness are exhausting. People who advocate the healing transformation of getting it all out in the open have never stood in a high school gym filled with misery. I sit on the floor, searching for a logical process, but no system, not alphabetical, astrological, numerical, latitudinal, chronological, Dewey decimal, makes sense of this chaos.

I walk into the hall and drop a dime into the pay phone and call Sam.

"I found a drawing. I think someone is going to toaster themselves in a bathtub."

Sam exhales.

"Sam, I can't do this."

"Be there soon," he says.

Sam hangs up, but I stand in the hallway, receiver in hand, until his truck pulls in to the circular driveway, and then I hang up the phone, and we walk into the gym together.

It's the first time he's seen everything unpacked. "It's so much . . ." He walks up and down the bleachers, inspecting. "Is that a taxidermy beaver?"

I nod.

"What the hell have I done?" I ask.

He shrugs his shoulders, reaches in his jacket pocket, and pulls out a flask. He puts his arm around my shoulders and shakes the flask like a baby's rattle. "Drink up."

"It's barely noon."

"And you're sailing on Shit Sea without a skipper."

I swig and wince. Sam picks up a half sandwich I'd left on a bleacher. The waxed paper crinkles, and with a mouthful of meatloaf he says, "This is good."

"Coffee?" I ask.

He shakes his head and instead swigs from the flask and then passes it back.

"Sam, I don't know how to fix anyone else's life."

We sit in silence as he chews. He wads the wax paper into a tight ball and shoots it in the direction of the visitor's hoop, but it falls flat, bounces down a few rows of bleachers, and lands on a mandolin with missing strings. Sam gets up and retrieves the waxed paper ball. "Ruthie, people are dumb. Most of them don't want to see for themselves, they just want to be told what to do. Everyone misunderstood you the first time, so maybe you just need to make them misunderstand you again."

"I don't understand."

"Exactly," he says. "And neither will they. Also you need to get the hell outta here. Nothing good has ever come from a high school gym." He shoots the waxed paper ball and misses again, then picks it up, and waves as he leaves the gym.

The night I broke my arm, Sam drove me home and helped me to bed. My memory is fuzzy, but I remember he gave me water and a pain pill, and when I awakened, he was gone, and there was a note taped to my cast: *The doctor said you wanted this?*

On my bedside table was a small cotton square, without the dignity of a collar or a cuff, not even a buttonhole. The residuum of Max was the size of my palm.

When I could pull up my own pants, I went back to work; and when I could drive, I returned to my storage space. The air was stale and heavy, booze mixed with the sharpness of chemicals imbedded in photographic paper. I stepped over clumps of images and between the rungs of the toppled ladder. I squatted and sifted piles of snapshots until my neck was damp with sweat and pain-pill withdrawal. I bent the wire hanger that used to hold Max's shirt and shoved it into my cast. I scratched and then pulled it out and used it to sweep out any pictures stuck underneath the couch, and that's where I found it, crumpled and caked with dried blood. I flattened the image with the heel of my palm and licked my finger to wipe away the blood, but I already knew it wasn't him. It wasn't even close. The photo was of a boy, eight or nine, wearing striped overalls. A boy. Not my dead husband. A boy. Nothing but a thin piece of paper that I had inflated with ridiculous hope.

Thinking about it now, I should have seen it for what it was—a cruel cipher—but just because I make a living propagating other people's visions doesn't mean that I'm immune to a mirage.

In a short life, photographs are a fraction of a second that everyone mistakes for the unwavering, time-tested truth. Photography captures life, and photography reflects life, but photography isn't life, because life is motion and photographs are moribund. People in pictures don't die, but not being dead isn't the same as being alive. I thought if I saved enough photographs, enough time, Max would turn right instead of left, I thought we could eat green beans instead of lettuce, but no amount of stolen seconds will ever add up to a living man.

When I was rehabbing my arm, the doctor told me that making a fist was the best way to regain hand strength. The physical therapist suggested balling up and catching a washcloth or a pair of clean socks, but I didn't think socks and towels were worth holding on to, so I raised my good arm above my head, and as the remnant of Max's shirt tumbled, my weak and puffy fingers struggled to grasp it. Sometimes I caught it, but most times it landed on the floor. It took longer than I thought, but eventually I stood in front of our wedding picture, and when my fingers wrapped around the falling cloth, I said, *I'm alive.*

ESTHER

I'm standing naked in the tub, drinking rum and Tab and flipping through *Cosmo* while lady napalm clear-cuts my forested nether regions. The back of the box recommended waiting twenty minutes, so I've set an egg timer. It's been so long since I've Naired above my knees that I forgot how long it takes and how terrible it smells. Whatever chemist invented this stuff must have hated women. If you're clever enough to invent something that can burn hair right out of the roots, would it be that much harder to make it smell like strawberries or green apples?

The de-hair bomb needs ten more minutes, but I need another drink because as much as I want to be chemically smooth, I also want to be chemically calm before my first date with Brad. I step out of the tub and pull my robe off the back of the bathroom door. I shimmy the robe around my butt, the belt wings around and smacks my thigh, and Nair flies across the bathroom, slaps the tile, and slides down the wall. Now there's a bare patch on my midthigh. I check the clock. I still need nine minutes and I don't have time to re-Nair. I prop my leg on the tub and inspect my thigh. I'll just touch that up with a razor. Besides, if he sees that high on my legs, the lights will probably be low. I let the other half of my robe hang off my body and drag along the floor while I walk to the kitchen, half-naked but full of smell. I thought the fumes would be better outside the bathroom, but the hallway stinks too.

Oh, right. The fumes are following me because I am the fumes. My nose tickles and burns, and oh no, not a sneeze, Nair will go everywhere. I plug my nose and hold my breath, but it's no use. I pitch forward and sneeze and slap my thigh by instinct. A whack of foam-covered and fried pubes plops onto the hall carpet. The carpet hisses and begins to sizzle and shrink. There goes my damage deposit. I slow-waddle, but Nair slides from my thighs and drops onto my feet like clumps of peppered cottage cheese. That burns. I lean back and tilt my hips to the ceiling and make my way down the hall until I round the corner and feel linoleum. I grab the roll of paper towels and wipe my feet. First date bonus: hair-free feet.

I refill my drink, and back in the hall the Nair has worked its magic on the long, rust-colored shag. I unroll paper towels, drop them on top of the carpet, and rub the mess with my feet. It's hard to move my feet without moving my hips, and everything is sliding and I'm depilatoring areas that shouldn't be depilatoried, and the Nair is dissolving the paper towels, and what's left of the shag is stuck to my feet. The egg timer goes off. This must be why the box recommended, *Don't move while product is working.* All I wanted to do was tame the tufts of my hair poufing out the side of my panties. I just wanted smooth thighs, but now I've got shag feet and a Telly Savalas no-no spot. Grown women are supposed to have hair down there. What if he thinks there's something wrong with me, like I've got a disease? I look at the clock. This carpet cleaning has made me late.

I shower and loofah and lotion, and as I belt my robe, chunks of pink chenille fall on the bath mat, more evidence of this Nair-do-well situation. I wipe the steam from the mirror and tease and pluck, prime, curl, contour, and blend, brush, mousse, and spritz. Am I wearing enough perfume? It's hard to tell. The line between just right and so wrong is thinner than the lead of a #2 pencil. Best to err on the side of smelling great, and really, one more spritz never hurt anyone. I spray and twirl and tuck my nose in my blouse and, yes, that's just right, I smell good. I leave a few buttons unbuttoned and slip on a necklace that's long enough to make Brad curious about what's dangling at the end of the chain. My eyes are still a bit red from the Nair fumes, but otherwise I look pretty good. I bend over, tease the underside of my hair a bit more, and then flip up for a last mirror check. If I smell good now, maybe with one more spray, I'll smell irresistible. A quick mist on my wrist and a low spray into Telly Savalas territory, and holy hell, that stings.

I step out into the hall. I've sprayed too much.

I can fix this. I'll just change shirts. I open my closet. All my clothes are on the floor because when I burned all my plungers, I burned my wooden hangers, so I wouldn't bite them again. I look at my clock radio. He's coming in ten minutes. Everything is wrinkled. I'm a lousy ironer, and even if I weren't, this is the blouse; I've got to wear this one. It's my favorite. It works with my eyes.

I'll call him.

I can't call him. I don't have his number.

In the trash room we laughed about how funny it was that we lived in the same building but had never met, and then he asked for my apartment number and said he'd knock at eight, which is in nine minutes. I didn't think I'd need his number. Maybe I can hide? No, he'd smell me through the door. Maybe the lady-napalmed carpet will mask my smell. Wait, is that worse?

Eight minutes.

I will make this work.

I run to the bathroom, take off my blouse, and step into the tub. I throw open the window, dangle my shirt out, and shake it like crazy. Brad is in the parking lot. He's cleaning out his car, shoving pop cans and hamburger cartons into a garbage bag. I yank the shirt back in the window and crouch in the tub. Did he see me?

I peek out. He's sweeping off the back seat and shaking out the floor mats. He hangs a tree-shaped air freshener from the rearview mirror, slams the door, and walks across the parking lot. As soon as he's out of view, I shake extra hard and then smell my shirt. Less perfumey. Success.

But what if he likes perfume?

And now my pits stink.

I grab a washcloth and wipe and then sniff.

Better.

But, not great.

Five minutes.

Not enough time to shower but more than enough time for one teeny spray, just enough to cover the sweat. I'll spray myself, not the shirt. Wait, that's where I started. New plan. I'll spray one pit with deodorant, one pit with perfume.

Three minutes. Time for a last mirror check.

My eyeshadow is creased from all the shirt waving and nervous sweating, but nothing a Q-tip can't handle. I open the medicine cabinet and reach for a cotton swab.

I swab my greasy eyelids. Better. See? I can solve problems. I'm a problem solver with a date.

Was that a knock? Is he here?

I check my watch and bump the entire box of swabs into the toilet. Toilet water splashes on my crotch. I've got toilet water on my crotch. Hundreds of tiny white sticks fill the toilet, bobbing and swelling, and my crotch looks like I've wet myself.

I grab a towel and rub, and ouch, that hurts, but I keep rubbing because a choice between greeting my date in a toilet-water skirt or enduring raw-crotch pain isn't much of a choice. I grab the hair dryer and aim it, but the heat burns my skin, and the wrinkles are stubborn. Maybe he's the kind of guy who digs wrinkled crotches. That's got to exist. Guys that like crotch wrinkles?

That doesn't exist.

Another knock.

That's definitely him. I slam the toilet lid, gloss my lips, and hold my purse in front of my skirt and try to act cool. I open the door.

"Hi."

"Hi."

"Come in."

"Can I use your bathroom?"

"My bathroom?"

"Yeah."

"I don't have a bathroom."

"You don't have a bathroom?"

"Ha. Of course I have a bathroom. I mean I don't have a toilet."

"You don't have a toilet?"

"Yeah." I laugh. "No. I mean of course I have a toilet, but I broke it. I mean it's broken."

"Did you tell the super?"

"Um, yeah. No. I will."

"We can stop by the super's apartment on the way out."

"Oh, no, we don't have to do that."

"Are you sure?"

"Yeah. It's fine, everything's fine."

I grab my keys and bump Brad out the door. In the car he tells me that I smell good. I nudge an old french fry to the edge of the floor mat and tell him his car is really clean. We go to Captain Macs, the lakefront seafood restaurant decorated with rope and old anchors. The waiter greets us with "Ahoy, matey!" then leads us to a table on the patio. We order an appetizer basket of fried clams and popcorn shrimp to split, and when the food arrives it's salty and hot, and the beer is cold, and the lake shimmers in the late summer light in that way that makes me feel calm and excited at the same time. I cross my legs, and their smoothness surprises me. I smile as Brad dips shrimp into ketchup and tells me about his job at the lumber mill. He likes his job, and he likes talking about the hardness of mahogany and the surprising softness of yew. When he tells me about the big pile of miscuts, I drink to cover up my surplus saliva.

"You must be really thirsty."

I nod and swallow.

Our hands touch as we reach for the same fried clam. That seems like a sign.

"Just how big is the miscut pile? And where is it, exactly?"

I imagine a buffet of redwood and walnut while I smile and chew my clam. It tastes like a deep-fried rubber band, but I don't care. I love it. Bring me more crispy rubber bands. I'm on a date. This is what people do. They talk about their jobs and dip deep-fried sea creatures in ketchup and feel the breeze on their smooth knees. The waiter refills our waters, and we order dinner—crab cakes for me, halibut for him—and after the waiter takes our menus, Brad brushes my hand and tells me he's never met a woman who's so interested in wood.

We talk about the factory fire because it's hard not to, it's all anyone is talking about. In the soft clink of forks on plates and wineglasses on metal tables, I overhear snippets, concerned words and wonderings from people who don't work at the factory, because those of us who do aren't eating at lakefront restaurants because we aren't getting paid. When Brad asks what I do at the factory, I say, "Quality control," and he's satisfied with that. I don't tell him the truth because every time I do, bad things happen.

Those bad things usually go like this: The guy and I could be at a bar, or a restaurant, an outdoor symphony/movie/little theater production of *Camelot*—it doesn't matter. The small talk goes well, sometimes even great; there's laughter, and hair flips, and arm touches. I keep the conversation away from my job as long as possible, which is easy because guys are more than willing to talk about themselves, and even if the guy is half-decent and wants to know things about me, the few times I've been honest and said, *I get paid to put things in my mouth*, he smirks and adjusts his balls, mistaking the truth for flirtation. I use as many euphemisms as I can, but sooner or later I have to tell the truth— *I bite wood.* At that point they wince or cough and guard their crotch with whatever is close, a coat, a bucket of popcorn, the playbill. All pleasantries stop and its *Check, please* or *I've got an early meeting tomorrow.* Honesty makes it impossible for me to get a second date.

Brad doesn't ask anything else about my job, so we eat fish and crab cakes and look at the lake and talk about summer. He doesn't ask for details about the accident, but before we order dessert, he reaches for my hands and says, "It must have been hard to be there."

"Yeah, it was, but let's not talk about it."

He smiles and says, "Okay. Let's talk about our dogs."

He's got a toothy smile. Excellent incisors. I can't resist a guy with thick teeth, so when he suggests O'Malley's for a beer because his friend's Foghat cover band is playing, I say yes. Over the first beer we talk about how long we've lived in the apartment building. Over the second beer I suggest a game of darts, and as he holds the dart and readies his throw, I can't stop imagining the perfect white slopes of his knuckles underneath my teeth. Those tiny hand mountains, thin skinned, delicious and easy to summit. He hits a bull's-eye and orders another round. I hit a bull's-eye, too, so I buy the round after that. I win the next two games, and as he tries to catch up, I imagine wrapping my teeth around his T-shirt collar and pulling it over his head.

He loses three games in a row and brings the next round to a high table in the corner of the bar. He reaches across the table and strokes my hair and tells me he likes that I'm not one of those nervous types who pick at their beer labels. We clink bottle necks, and then he leans in and kisses me. I want to teeth his lips, but I don't. We drink more and kiss more, and I keep my teeth away from his lips, and when his friend's band plays "Slow Ride," he pulls me onto the dance floor, and I wrap my arms around his waist and make myself count to ten before I take the fleshy part of his earlobe in my mouth. The male body is mimicked in the size and shape of the ear, and as I teeth his cartilage's rim, I imagine his shin and thighbone. We sway, and I keep nibbling, previewing his hip and pelvis. When the song ends, he pulls me closer and says something about wanting to take me for a slow ride. His words are slurry and his voice is low; Telly Savalas tingles. The bartender yells, "Last call." We stumble arm in arm to the bar. Brad orders tequila shots, and I'm already woozy from ear parts and beer, so as the bartender puts the shot glasses on the bar, I hook my hands behind my back, grab the shot with my teeth, flip my head back, and drain it without using my hands. The crowd claps, and Brad throws his arm around my shoulder and kisses me.

We leave the bar, cross the parking lot, and he squeezes my waist as we lean against his car. He fumbles for his keys, and I nudge his boots apart and step in between his legs. I cup his elbow and hinge his forearm tight against his bicep. I raise his arm and spread his fingers until they grasp his own shoulder, turning his limb into a stiff V. Three places reveal a man's girth, and two of them are elbows and kneecaps. I rise on my tiptoes, hook two fingers through his belt loop to steady myself, and slide the knob of his elbow into my mouth. He's new to me, so I'm delicate. His skin tastes like bar smoke and denim shirt. I'm drunk-hungry and pelvis-starved, but this isn't a meal, it's just a snack. Brad looks down. A smile spreads across his lips. I increase the pressure. His skin yields and springs back, like checking a cake to see if it's done. He half laughs and whispers, "Easy, tiger," and pulls his arm from my mouth and puts his hands behind my neck. He's a good kisser, but kissing isn't biting, and lips aren't bones. Lips are delicate, and his are plump, which is sexy, but plump is fluid, plump is weak, and with barely a taste, I'd draw blood. Bone is solid; bone is resolved. Lips are for anybody, but bone is all mine.

We roll the windows down and drive past the Great Lake. The breeze billows my skirt. I kick off my shoes and pick up the hidden french fry with my toes and toss it out the window. There's no air better than summer air, the wind of coatless freedom and useless socks. I tilt my head back and watch the streetlights blur on the windshield. At the stoplight, I slide over and rest my head on his thigh. The turn signal click-clicks, the tree-shaped air freshener sways, and I imagine toothing the rigid circle of the steering wheel. I lift up to try it, but the light changes, and Brad turns the wheel, so I stay put and stare at his big belt buckle.

After a slow, wide turn, we're in the apartment parking lot. His keys dangle in the ignition, and he gets out of the car and pulls my body across the big bench seat. Under the parking lot's high yellow lights, he leans down and nibbles my ear. He's gentle—an amateur—because men think that's what we want.

Brad opens the lobby door for me, and I climb the stairs in front of him, each rise a showcase of pendulum hips. On the second landing he gets my drift and thrusts his hands up my skirt, and on the fifth landing, in front of my apartment, he hooks his thumb under the elastic of my panties and presses me against my door. After two more flights we're on the seventh floor, and he's fishing the keys out of his tight jeans pocket. I push him against his door and kneel, grasping his shirttail between my front teeth. I jerk my chin, and—snap, snap—his shirt falls open.

Brad laughs and throws me over his shoulder, then carries me down the hall until we reach the bedroom. He tosses me on his bed, and I can't believe it, a brass bed. Headboard, footboard, one, two, three, four, five, so many hard and shiny tubes. Brad kicks off his shoes, and I hear his belt buckle hit the floor. He crawls on the bed, and my skirt tents over his head. I stop counting brass tubes.

We roll back and forth. I've been patient. I've controlled myself all night, and now it's time to get what I want. I hook Brad's arms around the headboard and shimmy down the bed. I push up the sheets and find his feet. I cup his heels, gently tugging left and right. I start with the right, holding his foot and lolling his anklebone in my mouth like a peach pit. I flex his feet, accentuating his tibia, the breadstick bone, more satisfying than its slim profile suggests. I work my way up, paying slow attention to both kneecaps. He moans and calls me babe. He reaches for my head, but I lean just out of his reach. He tilts his pelvis up. I know what that means, I know what he wants, but he's not going to rush me, not when I'm feasting at the crown of his hipbone. I drag my hair across his hips and push his hands out of my way. Not a bone, but just as stiff. I squeeze my toes for restraint. Only nibbles, Esther, more lip than teeth.

RUTH

I take off my shoes, spread a blanket on the floor, and wait for my eyes to adjust to the camera obscura, because there's no better place to reorient yourself than a room where the world is upside down. I'm here to see what everyone else is trying not to see, the remnants and rubble—everything that once was and now is not. The smoke has long since dissipated, and recent rains have washed away most of the ash, but police caution tape still marks the factory's perimeter and shifts in the wind like morose bunting. I want to look away, but I don't because I know the answer is somewhere in the piles of brick and the half-exploded graphite vat, in the busted pneumatic tubes and excised assembly lines. I come to the camera obscura because its eye is unmediated, it shows life as it is, not as I wish it were.

Sight isn't insight. That's a fallacy. Most people understand that things like pirouettes require training, concentration, and effort, but if I ask people how they learned to see or when they last trained their vision, their answer is flustered annoyance. It's easier to believe that sight is simple and innate because the alternative is to recognize that vision is unreliable, blinded by intent, and swayed by whims. It wasn't so long ago that scientists believed biological seeing was the result of beams shooting out of our eyes and feeling the objects around them with invisible hands. In hindsight, it's easy to dismiss such absurdity, but right now it feels pretty accurate because everyone in town has conflated seeing and believing; they've forgotten that we can't see without something external to ourselves.

When Sam was first learning to take pictures, he was obsessed with photography's technical side. That's not uncommon: amateurs often assume good photography happens because of good gear. They use reductionist logic: *How big is your lens, and how fast is your motor drive?* But professionals know that photography isn't about gear, it's about shifting perspective, and when professionals meet each other they don't talk about lenses. They stare at one another and wonder: *How does she look? How does he see?* Photography is like everything else—it's not what you've got, it's how you use it. Before I taught Sam anything technical, I taught him how to see.

He was a teenager when we walked around for months, no cameras around our necks, no film tucked in our pockets. We walked the lakeshore, we sat in bleachers and watched high school football games, we took aimless drives, we played bingo at the old folks' home, and all the while Sam fidgeted and protested while I kept asking the same question, *What do you see?*

At some point during that summer, Max repaved our driveway. Something was wrong with the humidity because the driveway dried with a series of small bumps, a tar pox. I asked Sam if he saw anything worth seeing, but he rolled his eyes and then rolled onto the lawn, and mumbled something about everything being stupid, and fell asleep. I went in the house to get a beer, and when I came back, Sam was staring at the grass. He looked up and said, *Each blade is different.* And in that moment Sam understood that photography isn't about equipment. It's about looking beyond the surface to find the extraordinary within the ordinary, to help people look at what they aren't ready to see—the dead at Antietam; water fountains labeled "Colored" and "White"; a young naked girl, arms floating outward, burned by napalm. Of course Sam wasn't thinking about all that when he stared at the grass, but in that moment he'd stopped assuming he knew what the world looked like, and that's the most important skill a photographer can possess: the willingness to see as if you've never seen before. That's why I'm not getting off this cold, hard floor until I figure out how to see the factory and the accident.

Outside it's dusk, my favorite time of day because, even though this light looks muddy to my eyes, color film sees it as electric blue, and I love the daily reminder that film isn't neutral; film is inherently, chemically, biased, and this is the beauty of photography, it sees in ways we can't or won't.

I can't erase another woman's lipstick from a shirt collar because even if I wash the shirt a thousand times, the wife still sees the stain. I can't expunge decades of hateful words or yank tumbleweeds from wombs or make sisters see in tandem. I can't guarantee a peaceful transition or the absence of pain. I've been looking at the ashy factory and the accumulated piles of people's past as problems of evidence, but that's incorrect; it's a problem of perception. I can't reopen the factory. I can't restore Frankie's speech, but if I look hard enough, I might see what we need. I just might possess enough fool's gold and trapped photons to refix my fix.

I wake up and it's dark. I run to my office. The phone rings ten times before Sam picks it up. "Meet me at the gym."

"Now?"

"Yeah."

"It's one a.m., Ruthie."

"Oh, okay. Well. In the morning then."

Sam sighs and before he hangs up, I say, "Bring your view camera."

ESTHER

I blame tequila.

I tried, I really did, but everything was so slippery, and it had been so long, and my teeth are bossy drunks. I knew I couldn't give them what they wanted, and it was all happening so fast, and Brad was all "Baby, baby, baby," and he was tugging my hair, and I liked it, and I didn't want to stop, but I knew I couldn't keep going, so I did the only thing I could think of. I bit down, hard.

Blood must have been dripping down my chin, because when he opened his eyes, he catapulted his torso and kicked his legs and yanked the sheet to cover himself.

"I'm sorry! I'm sorry!" I said and wiped my mouth, but he scrambled up the bed and flailed his arms and knocked a glass off the nightstand. The glass broke, and his dog started barking, and I moved up the bed toward him and tried to explain. "No, no, it's not you, it's me."

Mouth wounds bleed a lot, and there was too much blood to swallow, and I tried to catch it in my palms, but my hands were shaking, and the dog was growling, and drops were flying everywhere, and I guess that made the dog lunge at the bed, and he bumped my hands, and blood went everywhere, and Brad saw it and yelled, "What the hell is wrong with you?" and jerked the sheet off the bed and ran into the bathroom and slammed the door.

I grabbed a tissue from the nightstand and held it to my mouth.

I knocked on the bathroom door.

"Brad?"

The dog growled.

"Brad, I need to wash out my mouth."

The shower came on. The bathroom fan kicked on.

"Brad?"

Blood dripped on the doorknob.

"Brad?"

I pulled my favorite shirt off the lampshade and unlooped my panties from the brass headboard. I zipped my skirt and shoved my bra into my purse and walked down the two flights of stairs to my apartment. I fell asleep with ice on my tongue and the taste of blood in my throat.

FRANKIE

I flick the top of the beep-beep-beep machine. *See ya, sucker.* I'm leaving the hospital without tubes and without speech, but with fierce spikes and stars wrapped around my neck. On my last night Paul and Farrah threw a farewell, so-long, and don't-come-back punk dance party for me. The nurses' lounge was filled with inflated examination gloves and streamers made from the paper of the beep-beep-beep machine. They even moved all the chairs and couches out of the way so that there was enough space to slam dance. Paul made mixed tapes, and Farrah made my hair extra tall and sharp and gave me a silk scarf that looks like the night sky.

On the way home I psych myself up to pretend to be surprised about the surprise party that Mom's been planning for weeks. She keeps forgetting that just because I can't talk doesn't mean I can't hear.

Mom's friends hug me and say encouraging things while pretending not to stare at my hair and the thick bandages peeking out from under my star scarf. After a lot of awkward hugs and flipping to pages in my notebook, I sneak upstairs to my room. My face hurts from fake smiling, I have two paper cuts, and my bandages itch like a bitch. I flop onto my bed and press a cold spoon against my neck, an antithrobbing trick that Farrah taught me after I slammed too much but still wanted to keep dancing. The spoon warms too quickly. Note to self: freeze multiple spoons.

#7. Pro: Mute girl achieves worldwide fame for inventing portable spoon freezer.

There's a knock on the door. I tap, *E-N-T-R-E V-O-U-S,* but the knocking continues. Talkers are so dim. I chuck the spoon at the door and hope that suffices for clear communication. Esther pops her head in.

"Miss Cellaneous, welcome home! Can I hide out with you?"

Her eyes are puffy, and her speech is slurred. I wonder how much alcohol is in the glass of ice she's carrying. Esther picks up the spoon. "Should I ask?"

I shake my head and touch the bed so she'll sit next to me. She pulls two boxes from behind her back.

"Gifties! Sorry I'm late."

She hugs me and flops on the bed. I untie the curly ribbon on the first box, and Esther removes a cube from her drink and holds it on her tongue. I raise my eyebrows, and she rolls her eyes. "Tequila."

I pat her on the head and then rip off the wrapping paper. Inside the first box is a fudge-glazed donut, a picture of a life preserver, an orange button, a plastic ring from a gumball machine, and a roll of butter rum Life Savers. I reach for my notepad, but Esther stops me.

"They're all things that are better because of holes! What's a donut without a hole? A button can't button without a buttonhole, a ring without a hole isn't a ring, and you can't loop your arms through a life preserver without the hole. The Life Savers are in case your throat hole has a sweet tooth."

I wrap my arms around her, and she pats my stiff hair. "Impressive height. Open the other box."

The second box is smaller, and inside it is a shiny metal hole punch.

"So you can get even with the world," Esther says.

I jump up and down on the bed and look around the room for something to hole punch. Esther ices her tongue while I punch holes in a chemistry pop quiz that I failed, a *Seventeen* magazine, and my pillowcase. I open my window and empty the small drawer where the punches collect. Tiny *o*'s fall onto the front yard.

Esther hangs out for a while and tells me about her date, and when she gets to the part about going to a bar to see a Foghat cover band, I nearly hole punch my own tongue. I grab my notebook and scribble, *Foghat COVER BAND?* She laughs and grabs my pencil and starts singing "Slow Ride," but after one verse, she gets teary and drops the pencil microphone onto the bed. I ask if she will see Brad again, but she shakes her head, so I decide to not ask for details about her tongue injury. Instead, I unwrap the Life Savers and put two butter-rum holes in her palm.

When Esther leaves, the party is still going. I sit at the top of the stairs and listen to glugging wine bottles and silver tongs scraping in the ice bucket. Conversations drift up the stairs. "It's not your fault . . . ," ". . . with good rehab . . . ," ". . . she's young . . ." Mom is crying.

I plug my ears and walk to the bathroom. The only solution is a tub full of bubbles. As the tub fills, I look at myself in the mirror. The doctors told me I could remove my bandages whenever I wanted, but I've gotten used to them: they make me feel protected. I can't remember what it feels like to walk around naked-necked. I prop my head against some folded towels and ease into the tub. Bubbles spill over the edge. I hear the front door shut and car engines start. Mom climbs the stairs and pauses at the top.

"Frankie?"

I tap my pruned fingers on the side of the tub: I-N H-E-R-E.

She walks down the hall, opening doors, throwing her voice into the guest room, the half bath, and the linen closet. I smack the water hard enough to soak the bath mat, but it's not loud enough. I bang my fist on the side of the tub, and then there are rushed steps, the bathroom doorknob turns, and steam whirls and escapes past her.

"Frankie! I was so worried . . . your window was open, and I . . ."

I pat the edge of the tub. Mom sits, and her shoulders slump and shake. I gather the loofah and washcloth for privacy while Mom pulls toilet paper from the roll and blows her nose.

"We need a plan. You can't scare me like that. Things are going to be different. I'm staying home from work. You need care. You'll sleep in my bed so if you need anything in the middle of the night, I'll be right there."

I ball my fist and slam the water. The splash reaches the ceiling, soaking Mom's blouse and plastering her bangs against her forehead. She looks at me, eyes wide. The loofah and washcloth backstroke to opposite sides of the tub. I point to the towel hanging on the back of the door. Mom's too stunned to move, so I stand up and reach for the towel and drip sudsy water on her pants. I wrap the towel around myself, tap her on the shoulder, and point to the mirror over the sink. Slowly and big enough that it fills the entire mirror, I write *No*. Then I walk to my room and sit on the bed, waiting for her to follow.

We fight. It's a long one because one of us is confined to foot stomps and notebook paper, but eventually we compromise on a bell by my bed and an open-door policy. When she agrees to sleep in her own bed, I pull out my tap-code notes and teach her how to tap Y-E-S. After we hug, I teach her I-M S-O-R-R-Y.

I lie in bed and hole-punch my high school yearbook until my wrist goes numb. When Mom starts snoring, I sneak downstairs, skipping the creaky fourth and seventh stairs. At my welcome-home party, I found out that the accident was featured on national news, and because of that, strangers from all over the country have been sending gifts and cards the entire time I was in the hospital. Mom ran out of vases weeks ago, but the bouquets keep coming. They're shoved into water glasses and spaghetti sauce jars. A rainbow of stacked Tupperware and foil-covered pie plates crowd the dining room table. The den is full of helium balloons that weren't delivered to the hospital, and the couch is a stuffed-animal zoo. I shove five teddy bears and one giraffe to the floor to make space for my butt. The coffee table is piled with cards, padded envelopes, and pocket-size Bibles. Underneath two mugs of stale coffee and a full ashtray is a legal pad where Mom has categorized *Animals*, *Edibles*, and *Bibles*, in an effort to keep track of all the thank-you cards she needs to send. I move a coffee mug and peek inside a small pink box with a Manhattan return address. There's a typewritten note on a card with an illustration of a woman's profile.

> *Dear Franny,*
> *Any gross disfigurement can be easily hidden if you follow*
> *our easy 17-step system. Step one . . .*

I stop reading after step three and use the enclosed makeup brush to begin a paint-by-number of a basket of kittens sent by a Bible study group in Omaha. The American Society of Amputees makes me an honorary member, and the Al Jolson Society sent a button that says, "Keep On Tapping!" No wonder Mom is exhausted. She needs to worry about reopening the factory, not writing thank-you notes for corn casseroles and makeup kits. I slump on the couch and feel something lumpy. I reach around and pull out a stuffed monkey with Velcro paws.

I fasten the monkey's paws around my neck, and together we get up and turn on the television. I tidy the coffee table into reasonable piles and sort through the big garbage bags of mail and gifts until I find a box of blank cards.

Card after card, I write the same thank-you to different people in different states for different gifts, and instead of signing my name, I use my gift from Esther and punch a hole in every card. I pat Monkey on the head. It's okay, people have low expectations of mutes. At the bottom of one of the bags, I find a Betamax cassette. I slide the big tape into the player and return to the couch to keep thanking and punching. I glance up expecting opening credits or a theme song, but the TV fills with Chuck and his too-much-makeup face. Great, a horror movie.

The camera zooms out, and Chuck is standing in the middle of a huge crowd at the mall. The mall? Mom told me there was some media coverage of the accident, but she didn't mention anything about the mall. Chuck explains that the crowd has been waiting in line for days for a chance to fix their past.

I walk to the TV and press Monkey's paw against the screen. We touch factory workers in their color-coded jumpsuits and a man holding a big sewing machine. Everyone holds something, but all their somethings are so different that I can't make sense of what they're holding or why they are holding it. I haven't read or seen any of the news coverage about the accident because the doctors said I should *focus on healing*, which Mom interpreted as a total information blackout. I let my eyes unfocus so that the screen becomes blobs of clothes and faces. It looks like the entire town is crammed inside the food court. I see the hot-pretzel guy. I'd like a hot pretzel right now. Something at the top of the screen catches my eye: a woman clutching a scrap of purple cloth. I press my nose to the screen. Is that the *G* from the Girls! Do Work! banner? I rub my eye with Monkey's paw and look again. Holy shit. She's tried to disguise herself with a bad wig and dark glasses, but she can't hide Bubbe's watch, the one she wears every day.

I run into the hall and call Noah.

"Hello?"

I push "Play" on the tape of prerecorded messages that the speech therapist suggested Mom and I use to communicate.

"I'd like to order a large mushroom pizza."

"Hello?"

I fast-forward. "Please lube my neck hole."

"Frankie? What's up?" Noah laughs.

M-A-L-L.

"Oh, that. The troop sold lemonade to people waiting in line. Fixing your past is dumb. It doesn't even work that way."

M-O-M M-A-L-L.

"Your mom was at the mall?"

Y-E-S.

"How do you know?"

T-A-P-E.

"Didn't people notice her?"

W-I-G.

"You know that whole mall thing is over, right? That tape must be old."

W-E-I-R-D.

"Take the tape out, okay? It's stupid. You wanna watch a movie?"

O-K.

We turn our TVs to the same channel and watch the *Late Late Movie* about a weatherman with a drinking problem who falls into a tiger's cage during a live weather report at the zoo. During the first commercial Noah says, "I miss you." In the middle of the movie, the tiger scalps the weatherman, but it's so dumb Noah and I can't stop laughing, and it's almost like he's here on the couch with me, except he can't hear me laugh because I'm still not making throat noises, so I snap into the phone, and Noah gets it. By the end of the movie, the weatherman's hair has almost grown back.

H-E N-E-E-D-S F-A-R-R-A-H.

Noah laughs and says, "Your hair is cuter than the weatherman's." I snap until my fingers sting.

Monkey and I skip over the squeaky fourth and seventh stairs and pause outside Mom's room. I listen to her breathing to make sure she's asleep, and then I slide down the wall and tap into the carpet. I imagine the sound of my voice as I dig my fingers into the shag: *You don't need to fix anything. I'm fine. Go back to work.*

ESTHER

Brad won't return my calls.

No job, no boyfriend, and my tongue is so swollen that I can't chew.

Last night I drained the rum, toothed an extension cord, and nearly gave myself a home perm.

My period is late.

RUTH

Before the sun rises, I'm back at the gym. I unpack strobe lights, looping and taping their long cords to the floor so Sam and I won't trip. I hang and smooth the white background paper. I raise the big tripod and sandbag its base so there's no chance of camera shake. I move a table between the strobes and cover it with a large white sheet. I don't want any context or background, just bright nothingness. The setup is makeshift, and the gym isn't ideal, but I think this will work.

Sam walks in bleary from overwork. He's carrying his large black camera case.

"Sorry about the late-night call."

"At least you didn't break anything . . ."

He smiles and pats the side of the heavy case. "Are we doing what I think we're doing?"

I nod and pour him coffee from my thermos.

He takes a long sip and looks at me over the lip of the mug. "Ruthie, this is going to take—"

"I know."

"It's so much crap. Are you sure you don't want to shoot them small, on 35 mm?"

I shake my head. "The pictures need to be big, and they need to be in color."

Sam picks up a prom dress and then a bowling pin.

I walk over to him, and we clink coffee cups. "I'll buy the food and coffee and—"

"And beer?"

"And beer."

He squeezes my shoulder. "You bring it and I'll shoot it."

Most people use lightweight cameras that shoot 35 mm film. You can sling those cameras around your neck, and the roll of film is small enough to tuck into a shirt pocket. A view camera is the opposite: it's heavy and clunky, laborious to set up and slow to use. The film is big, 8 × 10 inches. The camera shoots only one piece of film at a time, and to expose the film, you must wrap a dark cloth around your head and focus on an image that's upside down and backward. This isn't point-and-shoot convenience; this is lug, position, and ponder. Slow and sustained looking, vision shrouded in rigor. Large format cameras were the earliest photographic devices. The kind men carried on horseback and used to document the unexplored West. As Sam prepares his camera, I think about that lineage because, even though we're standing in a high school gym, we are exploring uncharted territory. I asked Sam to shoot with this type of camera because it can produce images of infinite focus. Human eyes can't do that. We have to choose whether to focus on something up close or far away, but the camera isn't biologically yoked, so it can produce images of aggressive clarity, and that's what the town needs. We need to shift our focus, we need to see solid material objects that reflect light.

Sam is using positive film, so when the images are developed they will resemble large glowing projections like giant vacation slides or portable television screens. We're using a bright white background because I want the images to be simple and crisp, no room for distraction or misinterpretation.

Max couldn't explain excess gravity, but I know it's here, in this gym, and I'm going to use it because the force that dropped an apple on Newton's head is the same force that keeps the planets from falling out of the sky and killing us all. Sam and I are going to stay in this gym full of excess gravity until every object has been shot. We're going to spend days stopping the fastest thing on earth like it's a reasonable thing to do. People surrendered objects leaden with sadness, but what I'll return are images blasted with light, radiant and featherweight.

Sam wraps the photographer's black cloth around his head and shoulders and begins focusing on the first object—a floral teapot with a chipped spout. Sam checks the light meter and the strobes fire. He lifts the cloth. "Want to see?"

I wrap the black cloth around my head and adjust to the glowing glass of the camera's back. The teapot is upside down and backward, just like standing inside the camera obscura. Against the white background, every rose and leaf is sharp. I return the cloth to Sam. "This just might work."

Sam disappears under the cloth. The gym fills with a blast of artificial lightning. Sometimes you have to make your own weather. He lifts the corner of the cloth. "One down."

ESTHER

I've got cramps.

I root through my cupboards hoping for potato chips or Cheese Ballz but all I find is a box of fettuccini. I dump the raw noodles on a plate, and when the plate is empty, I gnaw the box. The stiff cardboard makes me think of Brad, and thinking of Brad makes me cry.

It takes a long time to stop crying, but it takes even longer to floss "Taste of Italy" cardboard out of my teeth.

FRANKIE

Mom wakes me up to tell me she's running errands and won't be home for a few hours. "I left pureed zucchini in the fridge if you get hungry. Don't do anything, just rest. Are you sure you're okay by yourself?" I nod and hug her, and as soon as her car turns the corner, I run downstairs and call Noah's house. I use our signal of letting the phone ring once and then hanging up. I finish five thank-you cards and pace around the house, waiting for Noah to show up and beached whale me.

Beached whale is what I call it when Noah lays on top of me, and we press all our parts, even the tops of our feet, together. Noah was hesitant the first time we did it because he thought I couldn't handle all his weight, but all his weight is all I want. I want something to force my shoulders and back and legs into the couch because when he beaches me, my brain finally shuts up. No one can hear me, but all I hear is noise, and all I want is silence. The silence of being pushed through the sofa, through the hardwood floors, beyond the basement, not stopping until I reach the hot middle of this round earth. Beached whale is the opposite of how I feel most of the time—like I'm about to float away.

I go outside and wait on the front porch swing. Noah rounds the corner on his bike, drops it on the front lawn, and bounds up the front steps holding a box of Fruity Rings cereal. He kisses me and nods to my head. "Impressive height." I smile and tap the side of the cereal box.

"An alternative to zucchini slurry," he says.

Noah lifts me up and puts my feet on top of his, and we zombie-walk into the dining room. He gasps at the dining room table full of baked stuff. He lifts off aluminum foil lids and throws them like Frisbees.

"Cherry! Apple! Peach!"

There are so many baked goods and casseroles that I've stopped thinking of pies as anything other than thank-you notes waiting to be written, but Noah makes everything fun.

"Ice cream?"

I pick up a cherry pie and tap Y-E-S on the side of the tin. We run into the kitchen and Noah hoists me onto the counter.

"Spoons?"

I point to the spoon drawer.

"Blender?"

I wad up a dish towel and throw it against the blender cupboard.

"Nice shot."

I tap, T-H-A-N-K Y-O-U against the sink.

Noah scoops hunks of pie and ice cream into the blender and fills the rest of it with Fruity Rings cereal.

"Frappé or liquefy?"

I stretch my leg, point my toe, and push the "Liquefy" button. The blender whirls. Noah tastes and then adds more ice cream.

"Cups?"

I point to the cupboard behind my head. He leans in and brushes my cheek and pulls out two cups. He pours our cherry-pie-ice-cream-Fruity-Rings shake.

"Straws?"

I point to the straw holder, a new fixture on the kitchen counter. At this point I can consume anything as long as it fits through a straw. Noah plops a red-and-white loop-de-loop straw into my cup.

"Where shall we dine?"

I reach for his hand, jump from the counter, and take him into the den.

I look at my bare feet on the carpet and turn to get my tap shoes, but Noah puts my hand against his chest. "Tap here." We sprawl on the couch, drinking liquefied pie and swatting at balloon strings that float over our heads. Noah slurps the last of his shake and picks up the letter opener. "Close your eyes." The balloons rustle, then there's the hiss of escaping air and a deep inhale.

Noah helium-squeaks the condolence card from Joe's Tire and Lube and then the card from a pastor in Alabama who writes that Jesus is the only voice I need. Noah reads until my stomach hurts from silent laughing. When the ceiling is bare, Noah points to the heap of black garbage bags in the corner.

"What are those?"

I reach into a bag, pull out a scarf, and wrap it around my neck. People from all fifty states have sent long rectangles of acrylic and itchy wool, assuming I want to hide what happened to me.

"People want you to hide?"

Noah kicks a bag, and scarves fly out. "That's bullshit."

We dump all the bags and pile and pile until the carpet disappears. I wrap wide, stumpy scarves that barely circle my neck and long, thin scarves that drag to the ground even after I toss them several times around my shoulders. I wrap and wrap until I'm so neck-heavy that I'm about to topple over. Noah leans in and brushes my neck. "It's like kissing a blanket." I pick wool fuzz from his lips and then reach for his hand. We climb the stairs to my bedroom.

Noah's never been in my bedroom. I point to my window.

"That where you look at the moon?" he says.

I nod and take the end of the topmost scarf and put it in Noah's hand and then spin across my room. It unwinds from my neck. Noah opens his hand and lets the scarf fall to the floor. He smiles and walks toward me. He takes the end of the next scarf and spins away from me.

Scarf after scarf, we spin and pull, stripping woolen layers that mound on the floor. The last scarf is brown and scratchy. Noah tilts his head and takes the edge of it in his teeth. I start to spin away from him, but he stills me with his foot. He circles me, unwrapping my neck, letting the scarf brush my shoulders and bare arms, and when the last scarf falls at my feet, Noah puts his hand on the nape of my neck, and we kiss. I open my eyes midkiss and look at the pile on the floor and at Noah's blurry face. This isn't how I thought it would be, but I know I'm ready.

I take Noah's hand, and we walk into the bathroom. I open the medicine cabinet and pull out a pair of small scissors. We stand side by side in front of the mirror. I point at the gauze swaddling my neck and hand him the scissors.

"Are you sure?" he asks.

I lift his T-shirt and tap, Y-E-S.

"You want me to do it?"

Y-E-S.

"Will it hurt?"

I shrug.

"I don't want to hurt you. Are you sure?"

I trace my fingers along his ribs and tap, W-A-N-T T-O F-E-E-L Y-O-U.

Noah says, "If you say it like that again, I'll tear it off with my teeth."

I smile and point to the scissors.

"Yeah, you're right. These are probably better."

I watch in the mirror as Noah snips the gauze. His hands shake a little, but he doesn't slip, and I don't feel the scissors. Soiled bandage strips fall into the sink. He's down to the last layer, and before he cuts that last strip, I close my eyes. I hear the scissors snip snip, and then for the first time in weeks, I feel air on my throat. The scissors clink on the edge of the sink. Noah's lips brush my eyelids, and he whispers, "You can look now."

I open my eyes.

How can something so small feel so immense? My skin is pale and pruny, and the stitches are tight and black, a murder of crows on my neck. Noah kisses his finger and then touches his finger to my neck. "You're a badass."

I pull him into the dry tub. This time I'm on top. I'm the whale, and he's the beach. He probably thinks I'm crying because I'm freaked out about cutting off my bandages and seeing my stitches, but that's not it. I'm crying because I don't know how to thank him. I'm crying because I can't do what every other normal girl would do, which is open her mouth and talk. I'm crying because I'm not sure I want to talk; I think it might be better this way because I finally know what I want to say.

He pulls up his T-shirt to dry my eyes, and I tap on his chest, T-R-A-D-E?

"Huh?"

I pull my T-shirt over my head and then reach down and pull his off too. I reach behind my back to unhook my bra, but Noah puts his hand on mine. "Not here. I know a better place." I raise my eyebrows, and Noah leans in and kisses my neck. "Trust me, it will be better than this tub." He slips his shirt over my head, and I pull my shirt over his, and then we step out of the tub to admire ourselves in the bathroom mirror. I look good in his plain gray T-shirt, but Noah looks ridiculous in mine—a glitter iron-on of a boy giraffe and a girl giraffe eating stacks of pancakes while riding bicycles. The girl giraffe says, "Anything You Can Do I Can Do Better!" Her pancake stack is three times as high as the boy's. I bought the shirt last summer at the iron-on shop at the mall, and when I handed the blank T-shirt to the guy who ran the iron-on press, I told him to remove the girl giraffe's pink bow.

But, how will anyone know she's a girl? he asked.

Because she's better than the boy. And, she's wearing a skirt, I said.

What about Scottish dudes? They wear skirts.

I spread out my arms. *You see a lot of Scottish dudes in skirts around here?*

He took the iron-on and removed the giraffe's bow with a small knife. *It's gonna make her look weird, like she's got steam coming out of her head.*

She's riding a bicycle and eating pancakes. We passed weird a while ago.

Noah touches the glitter letters that stretch tight across his chest. "Why does the girl giraffe have steam coming out of her head?"

I trace the giraffe's long neck, the glitter stretched to the point of cracking. L-O-N-G S-T-O-R-Y.

By the time Mom drops her keys on the hall table and yells, "Frankie, I'm home," I've refolded and organized all the scarves by color, washed the blender, refoiled the pies, and finished all but a small stack of the thank-you letters. My letters are shorter than Mom's because I take advantage of the fact that no one expects a girl without a voice to have much to say. Mom makes dinner, a glass of spinach-zucchini terribleness for me and a hunk of iceberg lettuce and canned tuna for her. I know she's had a crummy day because she doesn't bother to scoop the tuna out of the can. I sit on the couch, and Mom sits in the recliner, and we eat from TV trays and watch the news. When Chuck's head fills the screen, I hurl Monkey at the television. Mom turns toward me, and I can tell by her face that she's going to say something like *Don't throw stuffed monkeys at the television*, but she just laughs, and keeps laughing until she can't stop, and somewhere between the lead story and the weather report her laughter changes to sobs. I pick up Monkey and fasten his arms around Mom's neck and then point at mine. Mom's been asking, *Wouldn't you feel better with that off your neck? Doesn't that itch, smell, tickle, annoy you?* But I always shook my head, and she'd reapply surgical tape whenever zucchini slurry dribbled out. Not until right now did I realize that the gauze must have been a constant reminder of her failure to keep me safe. She reaches for tissue, and I bring the box up by my neck. She doesn't like to look at my neck; I have to make her.

"Oh, sweetie! Did it hurt?"

I shake my head.

"I should have been here to help you."

I shake my head again and hand her the letter I wrote last night after I sat outside her door.

> *Mom,*
>
> *I feel terrible because I feel okay. I know you don't feel okay, and I don't know what to do about that. Please stop staying home and please stop making blender disasters. I've made my own breakfast since I was old enough to check the* Joy of Cooking *out of the library and look up "oats: rolled and cooked." Remember? You found the cookbook on my bedside table and said, "Joy, my ass. Frankie, if a man gets used to you fixing his food, you'll be trapped forever."*
>
> *I don't need breakfast. I need you to be the mom you were before the accident. You taught me never to apologize for something that isn't my fault. The accident isn't your fault. I'm strong because you taught me how to be that way, and you've forgotten who you are, and that's the one thing I could always count on you to remember. Go back to work.*
>
> *Let's both seize our islands,*
>
> *Frankie*
>
> *P.S. What do we do with all this crap?*

Her eyes move down the page, and when I see she's starting to read the letter for the second time, I take it out of her hand and wrap my arms around her.

ESTHER

The mailboxes in the lobby are the best place to check if Brad's car is in the parking lot. If someone walks in, I pretend there's something vital about Valpak coupons and notes from the building super addressed to *All Tenants*, reminding us that the *incinerator is for normal household waste* and *excess toilet plungers don't fit within that category.*

Brad's car is gone, but at least there's actual mail in my box. I slide my finger under the envelope's seal, and inside is a folded piece of notebook paper and a pencil fragment, stumpy and gnarled, no bigger than my pinkie. I unfold the paper and hole-punched dots drift to the floor.

> *Dear Esther,*
> *Thank you for the best gift ever!*
> *I have a gift for you, but you can't tell anybody, okay?*
> *Pinkie swear?*

I look out the door: no activity in the parking lot. I hold out my pinkie. "I promise."

The factory is going to reopen!
xo,
Miss Cellaneous
P.S. Will you mount this pencil? It's the one that
stabbed me.

I jump up and down, and *o*'s fall to the carpet. I turn on my heels and flip my middle finger at the parking lot. I've got my job back! Who needs a boyfriend anyway? Don't you worry, Miss Cellaneous, as soon as the factory reopens, and I have access to my tools, I'll make the best case the Wall of Bite Fame has ever seen.

RUTH

I've surrendered any delusions of divination. All I want is dumb luck.

It's my last day at the gym, and I'm standing between two long tables. On the table in front of me are all the 8 × 10 positives, and on the table behind me are the original development envelopes people filled out when they dropped off their things. The images look better than I could have hoped. I slip on white cotton gloves so I won't leave fingerprints, and close my eyes and select a picture, and then turn around and select a development envelope. I don't want them to match; the point is to randomly pair image and order number. I'm surprised how little time it takes to mismatch past and future.

Once that's finished, there are only a few things left to do. I order one thousand white helium balloons and five cartons of white T-shirts in various sizes, and I call the *Lead Sentinel* and place another ad.

YOUR PAST IS FIXED.

COME PICK IT UP

IMMEDIATELY FOLLOWING THE RALLY CONCERNING THE PENCIL FACTORY.

IN THE PARK NEXT TO JULIET PENCILS.

ESTHER

The morning of the rally, I use restraint with both Nair and perfume. I loofah, lather, condition, and lotion, and when I accidentally smear my eyeshadow, I remove it with one of the five hundred cotton swabs that I've safely stored in the hall closet. I finish my makeup. I knew all along which was the contour brush and which was the highlighter, and makeup really does take years off my face. One last check in the full-length mirror, and yeah, my new outfit looks good, *Woeful Valley* good. I look great in white pants.

I want to be early because I want a spot near the front of the stage so I can see Juliet's smile when she says, *Reopen!* I check my lipstick in the mirror and race down the stairs two at a time. I put my keys in the ignition and "Slow Ride" comes on the radio. No, I will not let one lousy Brad ruin a great song. New pants. New me. I turn up the radio and shift into reverse, and as I'm backing out, Brad swings into his parking spot. Is there someone in the car with him? I put my foot on the break and slump in my seat. Two car doors open and two car doors shut. I peek in the rearview mirror. She's blonde. Brad wraps his arm around her waist and leans down and nibbles her ear. I thought you were doing that just for me. You said you liked my ears. Brad and Blondie walk toward the lobby, and he opens the door, bowing and sweeping his hand. That's a move too? Blondie giggles and curtseys and starts climbing the stairs. "Slow Ride" ends. You can't just walk up the stairs in front of him; that's my move. The radio deejay says, "Remember, Lead, the rally at Juliet Pencils starts at noon sharp!" I yank the keys out of the ignition and run across the parking lot. I jerk open the front door and catch my reflection in the glass. I still look good. Blondie's giggles echo in the stairway. She sounds like the dog toys I incinerated. I lean forward and fluff my hair; a few hole-punched circles from Frankie's letter are stuck underneath the hard aluminum edging that wraps the front of each stair. I flip back up. New pants. New me. I round the corner. More giggling. My molars twinge. Screw this. I take the stairs two at a time. My heart is pounding, but it's not loud enough to drown out her squeaky hot-dog voice: "Braaaad, quit it." I climb the steps three at a time. I turn the corner right before the fifth-floor landing. Blondie is pushed up against my apartment door. Brad stands behind her, his boots spread wide, hands up her skirt, just like he did to me. I rattle my keys and clear my throat.

She giggles. "Braaaaad, someone's coming." She turns in my direction and her smile glints, metal tombstones and spit-coated yellowed rubber bands. He dumped me for a metal mouth, for someone with braces?

"Esther?" Brad says.

"Those clams tasted like rubber bands." I lunge up the final steps, clawing at her stupid metal mouth. "That's my door!" My foot catches under the hard rise of the last step, and the aluminum edging zooms forward, and I thrust out my hands, but it's too late. Hard metal trumps soft mouth, enamel cracks, someone yells my name, and then everything goes dark.

FRANKIE

Mom begs me to give a speech at the rally.

But no one will know what I'm saying, I write.

"It doesn't matter, just tap whatever you want. People will be excited to see you."

I drove a hard bargain. I demanded new tap shoes, and finally Mom gave in.

Farrah and Paul come over the morning of the rally, and Farrah styles my hair so high I have to lean out the window as we drive. Mom lets me wear my new shoes, combat boots with taps on the bottom, but she wouldn't approve my Bee Gees T-shirt, so we compromised on a sundress, and I end up looking mall in the middle but punk on the bottom and top.

The entire town is here, and I'm nervous until I peek from behind the curtain and see the troop in the front row. I kiss Mom's cheek and grab her hand, and we run onstage. Mom's speech is about community resilience and the unparalleled joy of a sharp point, and as she stands at the microphone, I say the words in my head before they come out of her mouth. I listened to her practice all week. She puts her arms around me and says she is so proud of me, but in my mind the situation is reversed. I'm proud of her.

No one but the ten Patriot Adventurers in the front row knows what the hell I'm saying, but everyone gets quiet as my shoe-voice amplifies.

When I tap the dirty joke about the nun and two peanuts, the troop laughs, and because they're laughing, everyone else thinks they should be laughing, and soon the laughter spreads through the entire crowd. Mom and I raise hands, and everyone claps, and then I run backstage where Noah is waiting. Mom goes back to her speech, detailing specifics about the factory and the timeline for rebuilding. Noah and I sneak away on our bikes. There aren't any cars on the street since everyone is still at the rally, so we bike side by side in the middle of the road. Noah won't tell me where we're going, but I think I know. At the end of the rally, a bulldozer is going to break new ground, and as we ride, ash from the factory floats in the air, and it makes me feel like I'm in a shaken snow globe. I brush old factory dust off my handlebars and watch it settle in Noah's hair.

My only request was that I wanted to wait until sundown. I used to think it was the stupidest, cheesiest time of the day, but now it reminds me of the times Noah and I would spend our nights talking on the phone. We didn't talk at sunset, but we made a space all of our own, not his space, not my space, a space that only happened when we were together, and sunset is kind of like that, not day, not night, but something in between that never lasts as long as you want it to.

We don't have a reservation, but when we arrive, the attendant tells us they aren't necessary anymore. She explains the rules of the camera obscura and then latches the door and leaves us in the dark. We ignore her suggestion of sitting on the bench until our eyes adjust. I tap, F-L-O-O-R.

"Yes."

Noah opens his backpack and pulls out a thick blanket, a bag of chips, and a bottle of pop. I point to the blanket, T-H-A-N-K-S, and then point to the chips.

"I thought we might be hungry, you know, after."

He spreads out the blanket and kicks off his shoes. I reach for the zipper on my sundress, but Noah stops my hand and taps on the hollow of my throat: W-A-I-T. He kneels in front of me and picks up my left foot and rests it on his thigh. "How do you walk in these things?"

He unlaces my left boot and then my right, and when both boots thud on the floor, he brushes his fingers against my lips. I pull his T-shirt over his head and let it drop at my feet. He puts his hands on my shoulders, turns me around, and unzips my sundress. I step out of it and turn around, and we keep unzipping and unbuttoning until we're standing in the middle of the camera obscura in our underwear. We wrap our arms around each other as the room floods with light. The lake is over our heads and sand covers the walls. A gull flies across Noah's shoulders, and I try to follow it with my lips, but it moves too fast. A cloud floats across my chest. Our skin is red and then orange and then hot pink and pale pink. As the sun dips its fiery head into the Great Lake, I pull Noah to the blanket.

When the women on *Woeful Valley* have sex, they always close their eyes as if they don't want to see what's happening to them, but I keep my eyes open because I want to see everything, all at once. I expect to feel things, but I don't feel them where I expect, and when it's over, I rest my head on Noah's chest. The lake is black, and the waves are white, and my scar tingles and hums, like it's trying to sing.

It's way past my curfew when Noah and I bike into my driveway. I untangle myself from him, and he kisses me, and says, "Split pea."

I scoot my finger up his shorts and tap, H-U-H?

"I told your mom you were coming over for dinner. If she asks, say we had split-pea soup."

The next morning, I stare in the mirror. Yep, I look different. At breakfast Mom tells me everything about the rally and then asks me about dinner with Noah's family, and I tell her split-pea soup is my new favorite meal. She offers to try to make it and then asks me why I'm smiling. I shrug my shoulders and keep slurping zucchini through a straw.

I pull out my notebook from the hospital.

#8. Pro: Split-pea soup.

ESTHER

A woman wearing a paper mask leans over me and rests her hand on my shoulder. "Don't try to talk, Miss Spark. Your mouth is packed with cotton. Do you know where you are?"

A needle and tube poke out of my hand.

"You're in the hospital. Your neighbor"—she flips through my chart—"Brad? brought you to the hospital. You fell and knocked out your front teeth."

She wipes my face. "Oh, there's no need to cry, dear. Dr. Sapperstein is the best oral surgeon in town. When your stitches are healed, we'll fit you with false teeth, and everything will be just fine. Don't you worry."

I try to close my mouth, but nothing comes together. Everything is misaligned. I look over her head. A fine powdery snow settles on the window ledge. Why is it snowing in summer?

"Doctor, she's awake."

The doctor sits on a stool and angles a light in my eyes. "In addition to the false teeth, you'll need braces to help realign your jaw, but we won't know anything else until the swelling subsides. Would you like some ice chips?"

I shake my head and point at the window.

"That's ash from the ground breaking at the factory. Weren't you at the rally? It says on your chart that you work there."

His hair and mouth blur as he leans over me and examines my jaw. The pain and the drugs make everything hazy, but as he shifts on the stool, one thing comes into focus, something small and stiff in his shirt pocket. One perfect pencil, a pencil that I tested, a pencil I helped create. The IV tube swings as my arms fumble, and I paw his chin and tie before I finally grab it.

I'm not giving it up, and I'm not letting go. I'm going to open wide and bite tight. The dentist might be worried, but I'm not. Not anymore.

RUTH

People stream into the park beside the factory. The crowd is chatty, ebullient from the news of the factory's reopening. They wait in line and share donuts and hug each other with nervous energy. My staff walk the line, handing out white helium balloons and white T-shirts that the good people of Lead slip over their heads without question or complaint.

We cordoned the park with a thick white rope, and before the event, I trained my staff to answer questions and to speak plainly and loudly through megaphones. Sam is photographing the event for the newspaper but also for me. I want to remember this moment as much as I want to forget everything that caused it.

Adam is in charge. He was at the mall the day everything started, so it seems right that he should see everything finish. My staff wears orange Vixen aprons, and they mill about in the park answering questions, quelling worries, and directing people to the tables where they can pick up their envelopes.

The procedure is easy, the same as picking up a film order from any Vixen store. The customer approaches the table and hands the Vixen employee the bottom tab from their developing envelope, and then the staff member looks through the boxes of numerically ordered envelopes until they find the one envelope that matches the customer's order number. If customers lost their stubs, then my staff will locate the envelopes using the customers' last names. Adam monitors the crowd and repeats instructions as necessary. All the envelopes are sealed with large stickers that read "Do Not Open until 4 p.m.," and I've asked the staff to be strict about this. I told Adam I was going to slip out a little bit before four because I want to watch everything unfold from inside the camera obscura.

At three forty-five, I leave the park and run down the street to my store. I close the door to the camera obscura, and as my eyes adjust, I see Adam standing on top of a table, shouting into a megaphone. I can't hear him, but I know he's telling people to open their envelopes and then hold the contents over their heads, because that is what everyone does. At four p.m., the sun is at the perfect angle to act like the beam from a giant slide projector. Sunlight streams through the overhead images, projecting them through the air and onto the crowd's blank T-shirts and the white helium balloons. The park transforms into living, glowing slides. Customers point and gasp, and some people laugh, and some people look puzzled because they surrendered a shoe or a mono-grammed pillowcase, and in return they're getting an illuminated woolly mammoth tusk or a silver napkin ring. I've bet on wonder to counter confusion, and I hope people see that their past has been transformed. I hope they can understand nothing is personal because everything is perspective. The park blooms with images, projected onto gravity defying balloons and breathing chest screens. People bump into each other because they are all looking up, witnessing their regrets recast as potential.

I didn't solve anyone's problems; I just created the possibility for new patterns. Inside the curved walls of the camera obscura, individual suffering is broken and reanimated into photons swirling across shoulders and pregnant bellies, balding heads, faces and fingers raised to grasp something that seems solid but isn't. People hug, and some swap images, while others marvel at what they have. The tailor who wanted his wife to lose a few pounds holds up an image of the dictionary.

When it was time to photograph that order, Sam and I flipped page after page to find one without underlines, and when we couldn't find it, I took matters—an eraser and a bottle of Liquid Paper—into my own hands. The blank white page gleams in the late-afternoon sun—a starched cloud, a salt flat of verbal possibility. I circle the room, looking for the oily woman who surrendered that dictionary, and I find her, near the bottom of the door, crouched in the corner and turned away from the crowd. She looks confused. She holds the sewing machine above her head as if the thin film has actual heft. She doesn't seem to notice the gleaming metal dials and the crisp red thread. Her arms slump, and the image slips to an angle that can't project onto anything. The tailor will never see his machine, and he'll never see her. The crowd flows around each other, and a few balloons fly loose and float up. Inside the camera obscura, they drag to the floor and disappear under the baseboard. The oily woman gives up, and drops the transparency of the sewing machine on the grass. She exits the park with her hand up to block out the sun. I keep my finger on her and turn to search for the tailor. He's tucking in his T-shirt and laughing with a small boy who's holding a helium balloon with a projection of the taxidermy beaver. The oily woman walks out of the lens range and disappears under the door. I want to follow her. I want to stay, but I can't. It's time for me to leave too.

At the airport I check one suitcase. As the plane ascends, I place the tiny square—all that's left of Max's shirt—on the tray table. I ask the stewardess for champagne, and even though it's not my religion, I tilt my glass toward the shirt, look out the tiny window at the clouds, and say, *"L'chaim."*

I've closed all the Vixens for the rest of the summer. I need a respite from witnessing other people's lives because it's time to witness my own. I keep my staff, and they maintain all three camera obscuras. They're open twenty-four hours a day, and they're free. Before I left, Sam asked if he could photograph what happens inside, and I agreed, but when he asked me to process the film, I said, *No, you can do it yourself.* I left him in charge of the lab on one condition, that he describes all his images in words, just for me. When he asked me why I just didn't look at the film, I told him that seeing isn't everything, sometimes it's better to just feel your way, to swap optic nerve for blind faith.

After I land in Oslo, I spend a month traveling across Norway, sailing on ships and walking on cliffs and marveling at the deepest, bluest water I've ever seen. It's remarkable, but it's not what I came here to see. In every new town and in every new café, people can't stop talking about the unexpected clear skies. At night I sit in my hotel and read the descriptions that Sam sends. The retirement home buses elderly residents to the camera obscura by the lake. They divide into two groups. The outside group thrusts their wrinkled palms to the sun, while inside the camera obscura, the other group cheers as their outside friends seem to defy gravity and age by walking on their hands. The groups switch places, and when it is time to leave, the residents board the bus with the vitality of the very young. Teen girls gather inside to talk about their dreams, but they're disrupted by clods of teen boys who stand in the hot sun and hurl buckets of water into the air. Even though the girls are lying safe inside, they squeal as water plummets toward their supine bodies. The camera obscura is especially popular on full moons. Sam predicts a baby boom and sends an article about Lead's first camera obscura wedding. The oily woman's hair is thick and lush as she stands next to the tailor. He made her dress. She wrote their vows.

Sam photographs everything from inside the camera obscura, which means his images are upside down, a true representation of how light enters the eye. Sam could have flipped his negatives, but he doesn't, and when the newspaper prints one of his images, they print it correctly—upside down—to honor how the world really is. Stories and images from the Vixen camera obscura are picked up by national and international newswires. In Parisian cafés and on Argentinean cattle ranches, on subways and rickshaws, barbershops and street corners, people unfold the paper and look at upside-down images of the world, and by doing so, the world feels realigned.

It's the last day of my trip, and the shadows are hard edged and determined—there's still no fog. I'm drinking tea in a café in Flekkefjord and scanning the international section of a newspaper when I see an upside-down image. I don't understand the words, but I know the image is Sam's, and seeing through Sam's eyes makes me homesick. It's time to go home, fog or no fog.

I finish my tea and head to the coast for the last time. I reach the edge of the cliff, and there is nothing but sun shining on melted icebergs that have been around since the tectonic plates shifted. I look across the water's surface and focus on the light because looking at light is simultaneously looking at everything and looking at nothing. I close my eyes and open my hand.

"Thank you. I love you. Good-bye."

The square of cotton falls, but before it reaches the water, a breeze blows and lifts the remnant up and across the fjord. When my little square of Max is indistinguishable from the big dead star of the sun, I turn around and walk back to my hotel. This is what I want to tell everyone who is confused when they stand in the camera obscura for the first time: *Give in. Let your eyes adjust to the world as it is—upside down—but don't worry, if you want to rejoin the lovely mess of the right-side-up world, just walk out the door, because it's all waiting for you, out here in the light.*

ACKNOWLEDGMENTS

Thank you, Frances Coady, for believing in me.

Thank you, Vivian and Laura, for taking a chance.

Thank you, Benee Knauer, for insights that uncovered the real story. S. Kirk Walsh, for guidance and editorial support, and Julie Lawson Timmer, who did not throw me or my early drafts in the lake. Shane Krepakevich read rough sections and has yet to mock me (about that). Thank you to Sandy Sabatini for enviable style, unsparing support, and big laughs. You are a delight in my life.

Sandra Rechico, you offer unparalleled laughs and colossal support through the daily, the extraordinary, and the very, very bad. Here's to a life of eating soul food in the car and having excellent adventures. Thank you to Mayme for listening and convincing me everything will be okay. To Bob for being the best Bob anyone could hope for; and Hadley, your mere existence is more than enough. Thanks, Mom, for being proud of me before I ever did anything.

When life kicked me in the teeth, Ze'ev appeared, and Dr. Murray showed me the way. I'm grateful for Aita's straight talk and the willingness to set stuff on fire, for Stephanie keeping me and my ass lights aligned physically and mentally, for Wassen for being herself, which is to say, a beacon for the rest of us (What Would Wassen Do?), for Kelly for love and grilled liver, Frances for getting it, for Shawna for laughter and predate picture hanging, for Georgia's razor wit and movie dates, and for Laura M.'s hilarity and unexpected kinship. Miles! Your laugh can get me through anything. Chris, your effervescence reminds me that life is a party, and I need to show up, lips glossed, and ready to dance. Thank you to Martin and Cynthia, Will and Lesley, Gwen and Lewis, Monica and Gord, Nancy and Ben, and Susan and Marcel for opening your homes when I felt like I didn't have my own. Immense gratitude to my long-distance encouragement squad: Jodi, Jarrod, David, Emily, Davey, Missi and Brian, Risa, Jojin, Joe and Kate. Special gratitude to Lara for epic potato-chip quests, Last Words, and unexpected sleeps in stranger's apartments; and to Donna, who shows up at the right time and says the right thing. I'm lucky to be your friend.

Thank you to all my photography students, for the privilege of teaching and learning from you.

Always and forever, to Dummy.